We Are Already Ghosts

UNIVERSITY OF CALGARY
Press

WE ARE ALREADY GHOSTS

KIT DOBSON

Brave & Brilliant Series
ISSN 2371-7238 (Print) ISSN 2371-7246 (Online)

University of Calgary Press
2500 University Drive NW
Calgary, Alberta
Canada T2N 1N4
press.ucalgary.ca

LIBRARY AND ARCHIVES CANADA CATALOGUING IN PUBLICATION

Title: We are already ghosts / Kit Dobson.
Names: Dobson, Kit, 1979- author.
Series: Brave & brilliant series ; no. 37.
Description: Series statement: Brave & brilliant series ; 37
Identifiers: Canadiana (print) 20230620515 | Canadiana (ebook) 20230620523 | ISBN 9781773855264 (hardcover) | ISBN 9781773855271 (softcover) | ISBN 9781773855295 (EPUB) | ISBN 9781773855288 (PDF)
Subjects: LCGFT: Novels.
Classification: LCC PS8607.O25 W42 2024 | DDC C813/.6—dc23

The University of Calgary Press acknowledges the support of the Government of Alberta through the Alberta Media Fund for our publications. We acknowledge the financial support of the Government of Canada. We acknowledge the financial support of the Canada Council for the Arts for our publishing program.

  Canada Council   Conseil des Arts
for the Arts   du Canada

Printed and bound in Canada by Imprimerie Gauvin
This book is printed on Enviro natural paper

Editing by Naomi K. Lewis
Cover image: Colourbox #47907037
Cover design, page design, and typesetting by Melina Cusano

Corridor

Summer came again: how grand it was! Helen thought, to have the warm sunshine on her back while lingering by the lake. Should she not enjoy it? (Was that not the purpose of the butterfly on the rock on the pathway?) William, Doug, and Mike—Helen's father and her two uncles—seemed pleased, too, with the quiet and the warmth. For time was, again, allowing them to be, to breathe, while they were together at the cabin. Time was allowing them to take a breather from history. It was a gap, Mike thought, from the inexorable march of events in which they were all entwined, the giddy lights of consumption. Mackenzie, the dog, seemed to think well enough of the 1990s, at any rate. The war had ended for now, the fires were extinguished. The Royal Commission was ongoing. Negotiations and inquiries were ongoing. The regimes of the world were reaffirming and realigning themselves. They always were. The world teetered: the world stayed upright. The main result was that America had again asserted its role, Mike argued with Doug, all the while piling on the debt that showed how flimsy everything around them really was. The Canadian government, in turn, would be slow to make any real change. At the comfortable, well-worn Briscoe-MacDougall cabin in Alberta, however, these things felt distant. It was August, after all. Jéanne and Françoise, the twin sisters—Jéanne and Mike were married—minded the children from afar. All six of the children between the families, speeding headlong toward teenagehood, adulthood. The children, as always, spent much of their time down at the lake and in the water. Jéanne and Mike's three—Daphne, Benjamin, and Celeste—loved the waters. The children had all come through the winter with growth spurts and the dawning knowledge that the world around them was the same as ever, but also that it was somewhat amiss. The kids, in other words, were becoming self-aware. They were becoming witnesses. John, of course, hadn't made it to the cabin this year, as Clare—Helen's mother—lamented. Her brother had been away this past half-decade: she had hardly seen him! Let alone had her eldest child, the one who shared her brother's name. None of her children had seen him. Clare was concerned. Was Michael, her middle child, growing sullen? And yet. The earth spun on its ill-considered axis, its off-kilter twirl through a heedless universe. It seemed that fate had granted them a small corner of a lake at a time that pushed toward the end of a millennium, with food and drink enough to help them realize that they were, in the end, happy.

1.

But, then, does that not mean that we are all narcissists? Clare Briscoe looked out the window: she caught the sun on the lake. That we hold ourselves in regard, that we should seek to hold ourselves in regard—is that not a form of the very deepest narcissism? A Buddhist practice, after all, she mused, seeks to give up desire in the name of self-improvement. Or perhaps in the name of self-forgetting. It could amount to the same thing. It would depend on whom you read. Mahayana, Theravada. She imagined a statue of the Buddha, then a lotus flower, on water. The sun glanced off the lake. Clare moved on the couch so that the light wouldn't catch her eye: she shifted her weight from left to right. She dropped her hand. The book rested on the back of the couch.

Clare thought of Narcissus, looking into the pool. We are so fond of our reflections that we seldom look to ourselves. Perhaps Buddhism might take us in another direction at this point, Clare noted. She thought of her yoga mat, of its smell. She chided herself for the conflation. What her son Michael would soon identify as Orientalism. Though of course the traditions were linked—Buddhism, yoga—if not quite the same.

The smell in her mind, in her memory, turned to that of soil, to her long-deceased mother's simple love of the narcissus flower, her dirty hands patting plants into place in the garden out front of the cabin. The cabin rendered once again suitable for receiving guests from the city.

Daffodils.

What happened to Narcissus? Was he turned into something—like in most of Ovid's tales—or did he just die?

But she hadn't really been thinking of that. She was thinking of a lover she had had once. Years ago, somewhere tropical. She could recollect, but she didn't really wish to place the memory. The where wasn't important. She remembered his size, his gentle but urgent press against her. She could recall the feeling of taking him in, enveloping him. But his face, his face was gone. She could weep for that loss! The most tactile memory was of afterward, of his feet padding the cool tile flooring on the way to the bathroom. The gentle slap, slap of the soles of his feet. And then he was gone. It was enough.

How moments touch us, Clare thought. The children should be back soon.

She looked out the window again. If she could paint, if she had that skill, the view would make for a good painting. It was a quiet place on the lake. William loved the views. Her grandmother had been a painter: her painting was slow, painful, determined. She said that she had once been happy with a painting that she had done, Clare's mother Daphne had told her. Clare wondered what it had been an image of, that painting. And why she could only be happy with one of her works. What struggle! Why do it if it so seldom brought joy! It was a long time ago, between the wars. It seemed to have been a different world. Clare remembered her grandmother's small, unsteady hands in the evening of her life. It was years after she had caused a scandal, bearing a child late, an unwed mother who left her home as a result. But more than anything, Clare remembered her grandmother's Afghan shawls, her quiet strength. The surname that they kept. Daphne had cared for her mother-in-law in spite of the odds: they were often together during Clare's father's long absences.

The first generation makes the money. The second maintains it. The members of the third generation, the artists, spend it. Clare read that somewhere, but she couldn't remember where. In the city she could go to her books. At any rate, she was maintaining it, she supposed.

The children really should return soon, back from the lake. The sun would burn them if they stayed much longer, she thought. But they are old enough to know better, more or less. Or at least they are old enough to take responsibility. The older ones are. It took a long time to let go of those habits of worry, the persistent patterns etched by the quiet years of steering the children in healthful directions.

Of checking on them in the night to make sure that they were still breathing.

Soon it would be time to make the evening's supper. To get the supper made. In the city she wouldn't have to do so. But it was a pleasure here. A warm pleasure. Chicken. She would make chicken. Alas a dirty word, alas a dirty third, alas a dirty bird, went her mind. Chicken. She would make chicken, she thought, her lips pursed, remembering the lines.

She had been beautiful. She knew it! She had known how to use it, too. She found herself with him. Clare had foundered in the first marriage, ship upon the rocks: it was unhappy. But both she and

William read. That was a consolation. Absolutely nothing to sneeze at! All these years later—and still they loved one another.

What is it. Mean. Potato. Loaves. She had made bread earlier. The pleasures of the cabin. There were potatoes. Roast a chicken. She was always happy to use the kitchen, the bigness of this kitchen in the lakeside cabin built for her parents. Gerald and Daphne pouring their dreams into this then remote space—remote from their perspective. Was that it, to succeed? Clare wondered, though she had seen it. And did it lead to happiness?

Narcissism, her other thoughts interrupted.

At any rate, she did love the cabin. It was a grand space. Not ostentatious, but very comfortable. Large, but not sprawling.

The children would be back. Speaking of narcissism! Their teen years. It was to be expected, after all. Swimming off the dock, sunning on the flats. The cool of the smooth floors in her hotel room. Clare found her bookmark, closed the novel. A peculiar bird—supper. She had been faithful to William, after all—almost completely. She expected that it was much the same with him, but she would never ask. Whom would such a questioning serve? At this point! At the end of it all, it didn't really much matter. Things had turned out as they had. She was happy enough.

*

Down below, at the water, the children were growing bored. John couldn't abide how the cabin didn't allow for the motorized playthings that the other cabins embraced.

Well, in fact he did understand why his parents forbade them, he admitted to himself. And, in his heart, he agreed with the decision to exclude dirt bikes and all-terrain vehicles and motorboats. But still.

Somewhere away from the water, off in the trees, his father William was making a ruckus, tramping through the dry undergrowth with the dog, Mackenzie. William believed in upholding the longstanding Briscoe-MacDougall ban on speedboats and the like, even if it was a ban into which he had only married. Not determined on his own.

John did find the restriction a bit of a bore. He was twenty, after all. He could handle himself behind the wheel. His training in Kingston had him more than prepared, should anything go awry. And yet, in his heart, he agreed, after all. Back and forth. He sighed.

Shielding his eyes with one hand, he looked down to his siblings and cousins. Michael and Helen, his younger brother and sister, were on the shore with their cousin Benjamin. John's other cousins, Daphne and Celeste, were in the lake. They swam toward the small dock fifty metres from shore.

All of this motion, John thought. Always moving toward, away— somewhere. They were no longer children in the way they once had been. Perhaps Helen and Celeste were, still. But they were old enough to look after themselves: old enough to stay home alone, old enough to tame their former fears of the dark. Old enough to be the fears in the dark. Of an age to recognize the depths of existential terror, yet unsure of what to do with that recognition. Celeste was keeping a good pace in the shallow water even though her sister was five years older. Still. John thought: all of this motion.

The point, John reasoned, wasn't a voyage at all. The point was to be able to sit still, to stay in one place long enough to say that you had done so. To say that the place was, in its curious way, yours.

John looked back toward the cabin. Its wide windows were inviting from the perspective of the lake below. The afternoon light was getting long. He had taken in a lot of sunshine. His mother would be making supper soon. He turned, ambled down the shore and toward the dock that sat there in the lake, tethered to the murky depths. His lanky frame, not yet filled in in the way that a man's might be, crossed the muddy flat, a sandy evocation of the granite of the Shield that crossed the continent to the north and east, the very tail of a coiled and slumbering lizard of the depths along whose spine they all ran.

*

On the shore, Helen, Michael, and Benjamin discussed the future. Their conversation grew fanciful. Benjamin held that it would be a future filled with robots, a future in which no one would have to work because robots would do it all, a future without labour or surplus value.

It was already practically here, he said. Almost.

Then who would fix the robots? Helen asked. Who would design and make the new ones? She was impatient—these were questions that needed clear answers. Always questioning. (She was imagining those old tin robots, all awkward marching and sparks flying. They didn't seem up to the task of running the show.) She couldn't decide if the scenario was serious or ridiculous.

The other robots, of course, Benjamin answered. Silly.

We are going to have to head up soon, John interjected. It's getting late. He looked over to his siblings and cousin. Then he waved out to the dock to Celeste and Daphne. It was a wave that bade them to return, but it was also a signal that they need not rush as they did so.

Why is he so commandeering? Michael thought. No, not commandeering. Brusque? In charge, at any rate. By virtue only of his years. How Michael both hated and loved his brother at once, a twist of feelings that he could not verbalize. Michael was soon enough going to finish school, then he would head toward more study like his brother. Though he would not go to the same university, he noted right away. Perhaps Queen's? That way they could both be in Kingston, yet not have to share a campus. They could walk along the lakeshore in the cold wind together, discussing the works of the important thinkers who came before them. Maybe Wittgenstein? Michael had never read Wittgenstein, but he knew the name and that it was important. And they would lament the state of the world, how fallen it had become. And then Michael would brilliantly show what was to be done with it, because he would have read Wittgenstein and perhaps Nietzsche also.

Mother would like that, he thought. The same city, at any rate.

Helen was still thinking of robots. Perhaps, she reasoned, if robots did indeed take over all of the jobs, then humans could be free to be beautiful. Could they then create more beauty? She was becoming aware of the lack of beauty in the world, of the ghastly things that humans did to each other, to other species. She had just sworn off meat. (She had only just learned that it was possible to do so.) Perhaps the world could be more beautiful then, with robots making things work. They could help with food, for instance, with making it have less dreadful impacts on the world.

Pesticides, herbicides, hormones.

But then what is beauty? Helen asked herself. She thought that she knew, but what if her idea of beauty was another's idea of horror? How could humans in a robot-run future make more beauty if no one could agree on what was beautiful in the first place? It seemed that there was a great deal of potential for things to go badly awry in her cousin's hypothetical scenario. She twisted her face into a brief frown.

Helen turned to look over the lake. Her brothers were talking now, and she had ceased to listen. Celeste and Daphne were swimming back toward her, and the sun was lowering itself from its overhead vantage point. The sun lingered in these August days. It was hot. The steady strokes of the swimmers in the otherwise quiet corner of the lake rippled, splashed.

That, Helen said aloud, though in a quiet voice. That's beauty, at least.

She picked up her towel and began walking up the beach, waiting also for her cousins to arrive.

As she did so, her father William stepped out of the trees where the land met the scrubby grasses of the shoreline. Mackenzie ambled alongside him, his tongue lolling.

What a curious dog, Helen always thought. So loyal to her father.

The sun is getting along, William said. He meant that it would soon be time for everyone to gather for the evening meal. Similar to what John had said. Have you seen Uncle Mike and Uncle Doug? He was Uncle Mike to Helen, Michael, and John only, of course. He was Benjamin's father—as well as Daphne and Celeste's. The two girls were now pulling themselves up out of the lake, seeking their towels.

No, not yet, answered John.

He would be the first to answer, thought Michael.

They went around the bend to the north. We haven't seen the canoe since.

Not that he had jumped in to answer himself, though, Michael granted. What would it take for him to do so?

Okay, William replied. Well: see you all for supper, then. Probably an hour, maybe a bit more still.

William headed off into the trees on the other side of the shoreline.

What was he doing? Helen wondered, both in curiosity and admiration. She adored her father, in all of his quirks. She loved the hairy dog who seldom left his side. These strolls in the trees—he had always done them, it seemed. The why of it, though, never quite seemed to make sense to Helen. They were walks that he always took alone, too (well, with the dog, anyhow).

*

Into the trees, William and Mackenzie continued. William was looking for the detritus of last year's two weeks at the cabin, the only time each year when they managed to get far into the trees—the only time they ever really managed to make a proper mess. The other trips were more perfunctory, a weekend away, perhaps with an excursion in the canoe. He turned over a life jacket left out since last year. A child's size. It was discoloured from exposure and ruined. It had frayed nylon and the foam was showing through. But William merely smiled at it, observing what the passing of time had done to the blue and yellow of the vest's fabric. Chances were that it wouldn't have fit anyone any longer anyhow. He picked it up and carried it in his right hand, away from Mackenzie: holding it until he could take it to the garbage.

William thought of the time that his uncle saved him from drowning when he was about twelve. Exactly twelve—he remembered it with clarity. At another lake, back in Manitoba, long before he ever heard the name Clare Briscoe. His uncle, who had lost his own brother to drowning, saw William flounder. William couldn't see in the water, his myopia disorienting him, leaving him unsure which way was up. He remembered the sheer terror. It returned to his body for a moment. His uncle threw him a life vest as though it were a simple thing: as though he hadn't had to think of it. William's father never noticed what had happened. His uncle fished him out of the lake and left him gasping. William held onto the life vest for a good ten minutes afterward as he lay in the bottom of the boat.

William and his uncle had never spoken about it, but William hoped that it had somehow helped to make up for how his uncle had lost his teenage brother. Somewhat, perhaps, if not somehow. Nothing could, of course.

But that life jacket, William remembered: it had been orange.

The trees around the cabin were where William set his thoughts aside, the quotidian concerns of living, the daily concerns of being middle-aged. No one had warned him about how constant the challenge would be just to keep his head above the water. How each day took a deep breath, a conscious pace, and deliberation. The data from work sped past him, ledgers turning into zeroes and ones on a screen, printouts that either balanced or didn't balance the accounts. The pressure of endeavouring to remain honest and true in a world that was anything but. When he thought of it, he felt tired, soul-weary.

Back toward the lake, William saw the bright red of the canoe flash between the trees, aspen and spruce, birches. His brothers were coming back. In a moment he would be able to hear the splashing of paddles in the water, the rattle of their voices off the lake, the August trees rippling. William set the decayed life jacket back on the ground. He walked toward the water, toward the lake's edge, intent on shoring the canoe and ushering Mike and Doug up to the cabin, toward supper.

*

Somehow, they all found themselves at the table anew. Clare thought supper was going well. The chickens—for she had made two—had turned out nicely, and the rest of the meal had stepped up to suit. It had been worth it after all, the quiet all-day labour of getting all twelve of them around the table once again. The hot kitchen. Clare looked with gratitude at her sister-in-law, Jéanne, and at Jéanne's sister Françoise down the table. Then she raised her glass toward them both in thanks for their help.

Jéanne smiled back: Françoise raised a conspiratorial eyebrow. They all sipped their wine.

Mid-table, William and his brothers were caught in a debate about the latest public dispute. Yes, but surely you must see—Doug started.

He will be acquitted, no doubt, cut in Mike, whose profession gave him weight, a say in the matter.

William started up, then demurred. He enjoyed his younger brothers' arguments. There was always something newsworthy about which to disagree.

Perhaps, but the question is whether he should be, Doug returned.

Irrelevant, Mike said, his tongue only half in cheek.

We live to survive our paradoxes, thought the younger Michael, his uncle's namesake, further down the table. It was a line from a song that summer, playing over and again in his head. He might be named for his uncle, but that didn't mean that he had to like him, or like any of them, really, did it? It was all just a matter of time until he would be able to live without paradoxes. It was a matter of time until he could determine his own day-to-day reality.

If only John were here! Clare cut in. She meant, of course, her brother John, who had stayed in the city, begged off the summer's retreat at the Briscoe cabin, his parents' retreat, even though his and Clare's parents had long since passed.

The table turned to look at Clare.

Mother must learn to control her outbursts, John thought. I'm here, after all, her son, flesh and blood, even if her ridiculous brother is absent.

Helen, next to John, reddened, embarrassed by her mother.

Clare's nieces and nephew looked up, then resumed eating.

Helen relaxed.

William leaned over to reassure her. Perhaps he'll make it up next time, dear.

Mike and Doug resumed their quarrel.

Françoise sympathized in silence from her end of the table. She was very fond of Clare, as well as of the three brothers and their arguments. She and Doug had in common, at least, their roles in universities. Her sister was looking at her husband, Mike, her lips slightly pursed.

Jéanne had more at stake, Françoise thought, being the one who had married into this family, these three brothers from Manitoba, now all Albertans. But Françoise could understand—Fran, she was sometimes called these days, a short form that she loathed, and a result of being more and more immersed into the English cultures of Western Canada. She simply came along for the ride in this culture. She was a tourist, really. Sipping wine, enjoying the warmth. It was a large room, the wall of glass facing west, over the water where the sun was setting. She refilled her wine glass. The long table—two tables, in fact, pushed end to end, though a perfect match—fit them all with ease and comfort.

Françoise looked at her nieces and nephew down at the other end of the room, and at Clare and William's children, too. The conversation had resumed, breaking down into smaller exchanges along the table. She sipped, looked out the window. Then she caught Helen's eye. Helen, too, was at that moment outside of the conversation. What did Helen think of? Françoise thought. Helen was thirteen. Françoise tried to remember herself at that age, arguing with her twin sister, just before anyone else intruded into their lives. She would have been reading, perhaps, or else thinking about a book. Perhaps writing, one of those endless notebooks that she had filled with her looping, angular script. She would have been sad, though yet to encounter the despair or the sorrow of profound loss. She was young then and living in Montréal, at an age when she and her sister could roam the neighbourhoods from Outremont to Little Italy and down Saint-Laurent.

She had no idea, really, of what Helen was thinking.

Helen was both content and bored at once. The setting sun over the lake appealed to her, but she was growing restless. She hoped for no more outbursts from her mother. For a moment, she wondered what they would do tomorrow, but then she set that wonder aside. (It would come, wouldn't it? Tomorrow, that is.) It would be another day at the cabin. She held that notion in her mind, weighing it. It was solid, tangible almost, and, for the moment, unburdened: it was neither a good thing nor a bad thing. It was just another day at the cabin. She expected that it could be something more than that. And yet, here we are! she thought. It was the sort of expression that her mother might use.

*

The dinner continued: the family ate, the family refilled their glasses, the family picked at what was left of the chickens. As dinner wound down, the crowd at the table dispersed, bit by bit. Doug, who wondered about the existence of the table, about its very state of being, had almost finished another bottle of Chablis. He and Mike took their conversation into the kitchen, where they set to work at cleaning up. Clare was grateful for their implicit recognition of her labour, even though, every time, she never expected it of them. That they were modern enough men for their generation—alongside her William!— was a satisfaction that she harboured. Other women noticed the progressive household that Clare kept. She took some small credit for it, even if William worked while she led an unwaged life.

The children left individually, or in pairs, and eventually the sounds of a movie came up from the lower floor. The odd door closed somewhere. Toilets flushed.

William thought for a moment of the septic field on the other side of the cabin, away from the lake, filling up with shit. He took another bottle from the rack next to the table—the rack that divided the dining room from the kitchen, sitting along a low wall, a half-wall. The wine rack was just another thing. The bottle was a pretext for William to join his brothers in the kitchen, to refill their glasses—and his own—and to listen to them both, the lawyer and the professor, having their ritual disagreements. There was a consistent murmur to their voices, the splashing sounds of the sink, the clinking noise of dishes being put away.

At length, just Clare, Françoise, and Jéanne were left at the table. Clare moved to a closer seat. But there wasn't really anything to say. It was a long sigh at the end of a full day. The holidays were only really a break for the children, after all. The daily cares and labours of life continued for the older generation, as they do for all parents. There was, though, a leave-taking from their usual routines. There were moments in the sun or in the canoe that they would never pause to enjoy if they were back in their regular lives.

We'll need to get more food tomorrow, Clare offered.

I can go, Jéanne said, but I will need a list. You always have so much to do, after all.

It was true. When Clare had picked up from where her mother Daphne had left off, her mother's health failing, running the cabin had seemed to fall to Clare as if by nature, rather than by design.

But of course there was nothing natural about it, Clare reasoned.

Oh, of course, she said aloud.

Yet her mother had seemed to do it all with such ease, not with the impatient worry that Clare always felt.

I'll join you, Françoise said. It would be something to do, after all, the twenty-minute drive to the grocery, the liquor store. The drive was pleasant enough out here, or at least it was pleasant during midweek, without the weekend drivers blocking up the roads with their pickups and huge boats on trailers.

How had she managed it? Clare wondered. Her mother had been such a marvel! Why could she not do it as well or as seamlessly as the previous generation had? Yet perhaps Daphne had had her doubts as well. Clare remembered as Daphne had aged, had piece-by-piece ceded tasks to her as though—almost—she had been fond of Clare, as though she had never been able to see through her. So Clare thought, anyhow.

Okay, Clare said, for no particular reason. It wasn't, after all, necessary to say anything. Those were the matters of timing that the elder Daphne had seemed to handle so well. Clare paused for a moment, breathed. Jéanne and Françoise were old family to her: there was no need for her to have her guard up. Still, just for a moment, she panicked.

How Celeste has grown! she then said, a statement of admiration directed more to the girl's mother than anything. Jéanne took the cue. The conversation slipped into observations about the children. They discussed John's studies at the College, Michael's upcoming completion of high school, and the progress of the younger Daphne, who was not far behind him.

Françoise, who would never have children for reasons of her own, shifted in her chair, but offered her views on the children, for whom she cared a great deal. Benjamin, Helen, and Celeste's schooling, their progress in music, French, and sports. Each child had their own quirks, failings, and strong suits. They praised and fretted these one after the other. Clare refilled her glass and allowed herself to ease into the conversation.

William felt as though he could hear that moment, the instant when his wife let her guard down for the evening, all the way from the far end of the kitchen, where he had perched himself in order to observe his brothers' work and their argument. But both were resolving themselves by now. The evening was winding down. William could begin to head to bed. The children would take care of themselves.

*

Tomorrow and tomorrow and tomorrow, William said as he climbed into bed next to Clare not long thereafter. Mackenzie came into the room, harumphed, and began to find a spot near the foot of the bed.

Yes, there's always that, Clare said, until there isn't.

Mike and Doug had argued themselves out in the end. The case was, perhaps, irresolvable. Mike and Jéanne had retired to their room across the hall. Françoise had retreated to her book, something that she was reviewing for a journal. *Signs*, Clare remembered Françoise saying, weightily. Although the significance was lost on her, Clare appreciated that the journal's name was something meaningful to her sister-in-law. Doug's room, down the hall, was already quiet.

Downstairs, another movie was on. It had explosions in it. These sounds sent muffled waves into the walls every now and again. As usual, Mackenzie had been down with the children earlier. William loved how Helen rested on the dog as she watched television or read. He was a dog whom she had always known, a family member since she was about two years of age. She had known him since the beginning of her memories. Yet Mackenzie could always sense when William and Clare were heading to bed, and he always joined them.

How loyal Mackenzie was to Helen, William thought, and to him.

The sound in the movie paused. A couple of chuckles came up from below, Michael's.

Probably the kids are mostly asleep now, Clare suggested.

Perhaps, William said. We could go and move them into bed.

We could, Clare agreed.

They didn't move. The children were responsible for themselves. An array of pullouts, proper beds, and couches in the basement served for the children these days. Sometimes someone, or several someones, would sleep all night in front of the television. William, Clare, Mike, and Jéanne had agreed to this practice some years ago: they had thought that giving the children the extra freedom at the cabin might encourage them to like it a bit more, and that it might help them to bond with one another. The plan had worked well.

Clare stuck her cold feet on William's thighs. He suppressed a gasp. They pulled the covers up.

The readiness is all, Clare said, turning to face him.

To the last syllable of recorded time, countered William.

Mackenzie again harumphed.

Downstairs, John roused himself and headed to bed. He pulled the blanket up on his sister as he passed. His brother was still awake, his eyes drooping, yet still watching the screen. His cousins had all gone to bed.

Goodnight, he mumbled on his way into the darkness.

*

By the time the morning came, the dew had landed but then evaporated. The sky was again bright, the summer sun heating the air, lifting a thin mist from the surface of the lake that then dispersed. The adults were up first, helping themselves to the food at hand and settling in for what they expected would make for a quiet day. There would be no large breakfast this morning, the sort of thing that William orchestrated for some cabin days, for weekends: pancakes, waffles, eggs, bacon.

Clare set her thoughts toward the roast that she was planning for the evening. It would again take a great deal of time. It was very impractical given the weather. She remembered that Helen had become a vegetarian like Françoise. What about their health! she worried for a moment, then chided herself, letting the instant's fear subside. Instead, she planned for side dishes that would feed them both, as well, as she had done yesterday.

The truth is, Clare confided to herself, that there is a little bit less to do these days. The children had become so self-sufficient. In the city, too, she was noticing time creep back into her life, moment by moment. It had become possible, now and again, to stop and think. To be in the now, in the moment. The children would need to be taken to this event or that, the dog wanted walking, the house always wanted something, and William wanted companionship. In essence, however, life was becoming somewhat easier. Clare did not know what to make of the change. She distrusted it. Sometimes the recognition brought on fear, like finding oneself all of a sudden at sea.

What to do with a wonderful, sunny, calm day at the cabin? Once that question would already have been answered for her, either with childcare—diapers, constant meals to prepare, or just tidying up after the kids—but now the answer was not obvious. The children might need her, so she would remain in the wings, yet that was not an answer either. Yet how could one enjoy oneself while knowing that millions suffered? That the government was evermore repressive? That Canadians were turning on each other more and more? That Québec had very nearly left the country this time? While the fires of Kuwait were still a smouldering memory? Clare had begun to think of ways that she might start to contribute a little bit more to community life in Calgary, although she had long helped out in what she felt were small ways. But she was waiting for some kind of sign.

Auntie Clare—have you seen my swimsuit? Daphne was coming up the stairs.

Clare sighed in relief. Daphne didn't wait for an answer, just kept clipping through the cabin. The suit was drying on the railing outside of the dining room.

Daphne stepped through the half-stuck sliding door and grabbed the swimsuit. The door groaned. She was looking forward to a morning swim and to reading on the beach before the sun hotted up the outdoors too much. In her hand she held a paperback written by Leonard Cohen. She half-concealed the book, its brazen contents still perhaps too much for her—too much from the adults' perspective, anyhow. She found it compelling.

In the bathroom, she slipped into the two-piece suit. She then headed outdoors, pulling with her a towel from the railing, the same one that she had used yesterday. She blew gently on it until a small spider in the towel's threads was dislodged. The spider landed back on the rail and scurried over the edge.

At the margin of the lake, she found another towel and saw her Uncle Doug swimming in earnest farther out. She liked the powerfully built Doug—he was in his fifties yet was also a thoughtful academic who discussed books with her. Daphne had never quite understood why no one in the family discussed the fact that Doug was gay. It was a silence that matched the parallel one that surrounded her mother's twin, Françoise, and her relationships. Perhaps it was just a non-issue. Yet how odd, after all, Daphne thought—that both of her parents should have queer siblings—but not discuss it. It made little difference to her, in the end. They just were: Doug, Françoise. Uncle, aunt. Doug would not object to *Beautiful Losers*, she knew, at any rate—he valued artistic freedom above all else. She set the novel on her towel and slid into the water, hearing an engine start on the other side of the cabin.

*

Oh, there goes William, thought Clare. At least the truck is working!

In the sunlight on the other side of the cabin, William was backing the truck out into the lane. The truck was an old, battered Chevrolet half-ton, all steel and bumpers that had bumped into many things over the course of many years. The truck stayed at the cabin: it didn't suit life in the middle of the city. Nor did the plaid shirt that William wore this morning for the trip to the dump. At the cabin, one could let down one's guard, be less polished: one didn't have to display one's wealth: one could drift back toward a quieter, less fastidious manner of being, one that William associated with the past.

Just a few days in, and already a trip to the dump, thought William, a thread of guilt under his old ball cap, another piece of cabin life that never made it to the city.

Helen sat next to him on the bench seat. Curious, William thought, that his thirteen-year-old daughter would be the most interested of them all in a trip to the dump.

Maybe the bears will be out, he said aloud. He both hoped and didn't hope that they would be.

Helen adored the dump. As an excursion, as a chance to be with her father at an unadorned moment when he didn't have all of his daily defenses up. It was hard to decide what was best about it. The dump itself was exciting: a small, regional dump with a corner of dead refrigerators and stoves, a tip into a bin for basic recycling, an ever-shifting pile of household waste, and sometimes a scavenger or two.

Those who scavenged were most often men, and, much less often, women who were poor- and rough-looking, quiet under their hats. Helen felt an immediate sympathy for them and a restless sense of injustice that she didn't know where to place. There was something wrong—at a profound level—that such poverty could be the case. She would almost gloss over the scavengers, imagine that they weren't there, but they couldn't (shouldn't, mustn't) be denied, or ignored. How could such a stark difference exist between their lives and her own?

There were also crows, gulls, and, often enough, a few black bears. It was a small dump by any standard, and not enough for the bears to live there, but it was interesting enough for them to frequent it. The bears were left alone by the few hundred cabin-dwellers who used the dump—and this was more than one could say for how the human scavengers were treated—while the bears, in turn, let the people be.

Helen bounced just a little bit on the seat of the pickup, anticipating. The road that led off the property bumped and dipped.

I must get the gravel filled, William thought, but we always must. We must, we must. We must do something, at any rate. We must go to the dump.

At the end of the drive they met the road. The road held buckles and potholes as it wended through Cree and Nakoda lands. William turned right to head away from the lake. The road wound along behind the cabins that lined the water. It led them on a steady onward path.

Amazing that the province could pay for this road at all, William mused to himself. Dreadful in its inefficiency, serving the waterfront houses like this, meandering along. Yet, at the same time, these were all voting families, party supporters, donors. It made its own sort of sense. A steady onward path. Soon enough onto the asphalt.

It was the trees, however, that distressed Helen. Why couldn't they get more than a glimpse of the water from the road? After all, even though those cabins ran all along the lake, surely those driving by deserved a bit of the view? Should that splendour not be available to all? Or only to those who could afford the cabins? And who, after all, could afford them? The birches and aspens flicked by. Spruces. She saw one tree that had begun to turn early, its yellow-gold leaves standing out from the green all around. Motorboats hummed on the water, the noise bouncing off rocks and buildings, echoing off the forests.

The road led to a stop sign, and William again turned right.

They could turn left later, William thought, smiling to himself, after they had lightened their load. After the work was done. A full box of garbage bags, some remaining from the fall, nearly a year old. Some were the result of William's meandering through the undergrowth. The rest and the majority of the waste was the result of their short stay, however.

Ten minutes later, they were turning right again, across a set of train tracks and into the dump. They would end up doing another trip here before they left, William feared.

*

The dump opened up through the gate: odd and assorted mounds, the mish-mash of things that no one wanted any longer left like a ragged and toothless old dog at a pound. The sun was pouring down on the garbage, ripening it. Bluebottles buzzed in and out of the rot. The hum was perpetual, a chorus gathered to mourn the loss. The smell rose in waves, but it didn't overwhelm. (Helen rolled down her window.)

There were poplars and pines around them, or were they spruce? Helen wondered. At any rate, a forest smell tempered the rubbish. The dump was cut back from the parkland. Doorless fridges stared back at her.

And there were bears, after all. William wound along the ever-shifting drive through the refuse, compressed by the treads of the bulldozer that was parked in the corner, next to the trailer used by the dump supervisor. The bears came into view at the far end of the dump, next to the trees. The bears, three of them, were small black bears, juveniles, William thought.

Helen tensed: William sensed her tensing.

How clean they looked from afar, Helen felt. She was elated at the sight of them. Yet they nosed through the trash, picking through bags, tearing them open. Such dirtiness humans befoul the world with. What would we find in their guts? But they should be allowed to live and stay, she reasoned, for no one is being harmed. She watched their movements, the particular rhythm and sway of their ursine heads.

The dump supervisor was standing on the stairs in front of his trailer. He was looking at the bears also. Would he fetch his gun? No, he would not. Much dirtier he looked, Helen observed to herself, than the bears, whose coats shone in the sun and who looked lustrous in the shade of the pines. Or were they spruces after all?

For the supervisor was grizzled, unkempt. His light hair frizzed out at the temples. His pink skin had seen too much of the wind and the sun and not enough of the razor. His mackinaw (Helen loved the word mackinaw) was dirty. It was excessive in this weather. His jeans were torn and his bootlaces frayed.

Yet the bears were tidy, their snouts pink at the end, just a little bit pink, their fur so even.

And here we are, said William, backing up for a moment—Helen was jolted forward. Coming? he added, putting the truck into park, its old automatic transmission controlled by the stick at the wheel.

William climbed into the box. He began throwing the bags of refuse into the mix.

A fine shame, he thought. So much waste. If we are to be condemned, he reasoned, it is for this waste, not for any of our everyday trifles. Twenty-five years of banks, of being on the job, had taught him, if nothing else, that there were human trifles enough to go around. Use each man according to his desserts, or whatever the line was, and who shall 'scape whipping?

He threw another bag. One of the bears, perhaps fifty metres away, looked up.

Helen, too, stood in the box, though she knew that her father didn't actually need her help with the trash. This act was all part of their ritual, the trips to the dump that they were, by now, in the habit of taking together. It was, really, the only time that William and his daughter spent alone with each other. As she came into the sun, she felt it beat down onto her head. She should have put on sunscreen, she realized, imagining her mother's voice, her chiding. Her father never wore sunscreen, but then again he never burned, either. Chalk it up to a healthy childhood spent out of doors, he would say.

In the sunlight, Helen winced and then focused on the bears. The closest one looked directly at her! She looked back. Was it sizing her up? Imagining eating her? Or just inquisitive? The bear humphed, returned to its foraging. Surely it would come over to inspect their leavings as soon as they departed.

And with that, William heaved a final bag through the air.

The sack ripped in mid-flight, and Helen saw the remains of meals past sail through the blue of the sky. How banal, yet fascinating, the arc of this garbage, landing with the rest of it in the hot August sun. The mosquitoes were at rest, yet something landed on her arm. She scratched the spot: the feeling abated. Let it come, she thought. The itch was a small wonder, at any rate.

*

The mosquitoes would come out after all, Mike thought, from his perch back at the cabin. It was late for mosquitoes, yet here they were. Mike remembered, was remembering in the morning light as he smoked. The deck boards fanned out under his feet; the dew evaporated in the sun. They had been young; they had been sensual. Their youth was beauty, his youth with Jéanne. She was six years his junior. They had been lovers; they had taken lovers. They had, at times, shared lovers. Their freedom together had given them the bond that they still needed to be one, all these years later, twenty-six of them lined up like matchsticks. They were still sensual. His thoughts flitted to lovers, to bodies pumping and moaning. Dark fumbling: he recalled a lover on hands and knees, reaching behind herself to hold him, pull him, and then guide him into her in the half-darkness of a winter's night.

They had ceased to take lovers years ago. He remembered now with little nostalgia or longing. Yet it surprised him how it all had simply ended. Their lives had, perhaps necessarily, ceased to be about adventure and had become a more complicated attempt at something like freedom. His last lovers had all been unhappy women looking for an escape, and each of them had turned on him. Jéanne knew all of this. Jéanne was with him throughout, through the last of her lovers, too, and through the therapy that accompanied middle age.

He looked over the railing, toward the lake. He did not quite regret his last few, unhappy lovers, but he had for a time been unhappy, had caught the weight of their feelings. Or, rather, he had brought the same emotions to each encounter; perhaps the emotions were simply his all along. He inhaled, the smoke at his nose. He remembered sweat. He loved Jéanne. It was as simple as that. His conversations with therapists: for a while he had contemplated death. The thoughts, all of them, the memories, were by now familiar, though, and did not sting.

What had ended this struggle? The children were young then. There had been a strain. He was new to his profession and could not fathom the years that would lie ahead. He breathed; he sighed. Each year he watched as another colleague or friend fell for a younger body, for new flesh, and then suffered the losses of esteem. There were no solutions to life, just partial answers.

He looked out on the water where his children were swimming, then farther out into the lake. There was beauty and there was light, after all. The change in life had suited him in the end.

Mike looked down to the water. The kids were there. He and Jéanne had never known how to speak to their three children about their own younger years, nor about how they would be there to celebrate their children's coming into adulthood with both love and caution. He expected that the conversations would unfold, over time, as the children grew into them. He hoped that he would be around long enough to talk everything through with them. Yet every generation must find its own path, even if that path ends up retracing a well-worn one already laid down by those who came before.

Down at the water, the children, who were teenaged, young adults now, even, counting the cousins, were playing in the shallows. Daphne was reading on the shore. Mike's nephew John was elsewhere. Michael—the younger—Helen, Benjamin, and Celeste were dredging muck from the bottom of the lake, ancient glacial silt and mouldering leaves being pulled up from their repose. They were throwing it at each other. There was a mild chill to the August air, a just perceptible undercurrent.

Mike exhaled, then took another deep drag on the tobacco.

Jéanne slid open the glass door near to him and then joined him on the deck. The door was loud: it stirred him from his thoughts.

They seem happy, she said, the kids. You can hear them from inside. And you can feel it even from here.

Jéanne had just showered: her hair was still damp.

Mike felt a momentary surge, wished that he had joined her under the falling water. Her body still lithe, he imagined them pressing together. He loved her still, and he still longed for her. Yet he chided himself: why still? Was that how one put it, once one got into one's fifties? Still? It may have been against the odds: so many of their friends, colleagues, were divorced, remarried, once, twice, thrice. Not that duration was the only measure of a relationship, but it seemed to matter somehow. Look at Clare, Mike thought. How was one supposed to live? Had he not done the best that he could?

Jéanne still had her towel, was dabbing at her hair. We're going to the store, she announced. Mike always needed these reminders. Would he like them to get anything?

He paused, thought, but had no answer to give. He had everything that he could think of. The fact was, in itself, quite remarkable. It was perhaps more than he deserved. No, he thought, scratch that: it was what everyone deserved, but that so few had.

I wish that the children could be forever in this moment, Jéanne said.

She left Mike there, on the deck, looking out. He smoked: the deck steamed as the dew evaporated. The sun streamed, now above the trees. She slid back in through the door, crossed the top floor of the cabin, called for her twin. Françoise called back up the stairs. Jéanne descended to meet her.

*

When they were young, Françoise and Jéanne were inseparable, twins who looked similar enough, yet who also diverged. They knew the details of each other's lives, the intimacies, the discretions and indiscretions. For a long time, they had shared a room and were still comfortable sharing a bed in hotel rooms when they travelled together.

It was odd, Jéanne thought, how they lived apart. She remembered fall in Montréal as a girl, slipping her hand into her sister's hand, walking through the Plateau, down Saint-Laurent. Even though they lived at a distance now, there remained an easy familiarity, which was a blessing. But what she would give to feel that comfort of childhood! Jéanne felt that she could crumble for all of the sighs that middle age brought.

They opened the cabin door into the streaming sunlight. Françoise wore oversized sunglasses. She looked as fashionable as ever. She had done so ever since her uncanny childhood maturity, which had only accelerated after her departure for the States and then the Left Bank, a departure that had pierced Jéanne to the core, to the heart. She still hated her sister for leaving, for having left her: she resented her for having moved to the atéliers of French artists, for having been part of May '68 and for leaving her with the paltry consolation of Expo '67. For returning to Canada single, wrung out, successful.

Moreover, Jéanne hadn't remembered to bring her own sunglasses, and it was bright out.

They drove in Françoise's Volkswagen with the windows down. A city car. The air was not yet warm, but it wasn't cool either. They felt no real need to speak: they felt no need to rush to catch up. Whatever had changed hadn't changed them.

Françoise observed the day: it was sunny, warming, and sure to be hot by noon. As they drove, they passed John, who was running along the shoulder of the winding lakeside drive, the gravel crunching under his feet. Françoise saw sweat on his brow, could tell that he had been running for some time.

I'll be going to France in September, Françoise shared. But surely she had told Jéanne already?

What? Yes, oh, of course, the sabbatical, Jéanne said. Her sister, gone for a year. Again. Perhaps she could visit, make the flight over early in the New Year? Where was she going again?

Montpellier at first, Françoise said. Mostly Paris, though. I will be working at the Bibliothèque nationale for much of the time. I am so looking forward to the change. She emphasized the word so, underlining it, italicizing it. She wanted it to have an impact. I need this break, the shift in perspective.

It is still funny, Jéanne thought, staring out the window as Françoise turned left at a stop sign. We could speak French with one another, yet we never really have. Why is that? Even in their youth: English then had been like a secret language, even though everyone around them seemed to speak a bit of both. Their family had fallen on both sides of the line that kept Québec in such throes, and that had nearly driven the country apart. Their parents, federalists who viewed themselves as simple pragmatists, had spoken both languages—they were fluent—but somehow the twins fell to English amidst their French schooling. Even though, at the time, to speak English in the streets of Montréal could easily draw the ire of those around them. More so in some neighbourhoods. It had felt risky, daring, a transgression.

Françoise pulled the car into an expanse of asphalt, the parking lot adjacent to the grocery store. The store was on the edge of a town, with trees backing all around it. Early geese flew over, heading south. Their flight looked like one of leisure, but, of course, that wasn't quite the right word for it. There was a liquor store attached to the back of the grocery. Behind it, a small gravel incline led to the edge of the trees, the edge of how far humans had so far gotten in flattening the land. To the north, boreal. To the south, prairie. Here, the middle. Parkland.

For just a moment, Françoise resented the store, resented the fact that she, who travelled the world and was hailed at international conferences for her interventions into contemporary feminist theory, still had to shop at a depressing IGA in a stretch of rural Alberta. But then she chased away the thought, chided herself for her ego—and then felt bad, in turn, for her self-recriminations.

For it was a dull scenario, one ill-befitting world-weary global travellers: it was banal in the extreme. Ghastly. And yet, wasn't so much of the world? Françoise reasoned to herself. The asphalt was heating up, and a family—dressed in a mix of ballcaps, track suits, and jeans—tumbled from a late model pickup, laughing together. They all hurried into the store, which was cool inside. Dry.

The air prickles my skin so, exclaimed Jéanne, caught off-guard upon entering the grocery behind the jovial family.

Yes, came the reply from Françoise.

The women worked their way through the store, piling on groceries for all twelve cabin-goers—thirteen if one counted Mackenzie—enough for the next few days.

We will need more wine, too, Jéanne added, heading for the attached liquor store at the rear.

The store was drab, dark against and after the August sunlight. The other shoppers were also, for the most part, cabin-dwellers at their lake. They could be at the other small lakes nearby: Sylvan, Pigeon, Gull—all were not too far. Jéanne saw the laughing family again in the row reserved for milk and eggs. They were still laughing. The food in the store tended toward barbeque-ready preparations: there were stacks of condiments, chips, burgers, hot dogs. All of the related items that the store could assume would be eaten by the summertime demographic group. Buns. Carbonated beverages. Nachos. Yet the sisters found what they wanted, more or less. The store even had shallots, as well as bulk-sized bottles of sunscreen.

The load, including a new case of wine, fit into the back of the car. The twins drove home, Jéanne watching the leaves passing by the passenger's side. Aspen leaves trembled. Françoise hummed noiselessly behind her sunglasses, Edith Piaf on her mind.

Oh, look, John is still running, said Françoise as they approached the turn back to the small road that led once more to the cabin.

*

John had been running since the sun came up. He felt sweat running down his shirt, down his shoulder blades. He had already pissed out the water that he had drunk beforehand. He had shat in the ditch once his bowels started working.

His shoes were broken in just the right amount. The morning was clear and warming. The meandering lakeside road took him through a semi-domesticated side of Alberta that he loved. It was a space that folded in and out of itself. It was a space of willows, alders, saskatoons and wild roses. He would be back soon, was probably heading back now. He could, though, always just keep going. He had passed the ten kilometre mark some time ago.

Why was he running so? he asked himself. What was he running from?

The questions were unusual, like the uncomfortably loose bowel movement that he had had earlier.

Running from himself, he thought without thinking.

The rest of the children would all be at the water by now. Being the eldest gave him the freedom to opt out. It gave him the freedom to do his own thing. No one really understood why he had chosen, for instance, to go to the Royal Military College. It was not part of family tradition. His grades had been good, steady, enough to get him in most places. But he was able to claim it, head to military training, as the prerogative of the eldest. He breathed. His breath was regular. His diaphragm moved just so. He appreciated the discipline. He could now run for hours, it felt like. They would be by the water. He was here, running. He would go to the lake when he got back. He would swim out, dive off the dock, and float for a while. John would have earned it.

The shoes were great. He was comfortable. His stride had gotten much more precise. But why running from himself? When had he ceased to be perfect? His feet strummed the road, the rhythm steady.

So he was running from his imperfect self, then.

In his mind flashed the final moments of last year's breakup. He had struck her. She had struck him. The order didn't matter. It did matter. It didn't. He hadn't known that he would, or could, do that. It was a flash of shock and pain. He didn't know why he had done so, except in hurt. Their breakup had ended in desultory sex, but, first, he had struck her, as she had struck him. He had struck her once, hard, but had left no mark. Had he done so on purpose? Struck just hard enough to hurt but not mark? Could he be so calculating?

He was monstrous.

So he was running from himself. He would tell no one. To speak would be to be labelled. To speak would be to speak of his harm. There was no way to speak. She had forgiven him, she had said. She had hurt him. She had hit him, too. He turned it inward. He ran. The sweat from his brow was drying in the sun.

Everything since then had been an act. He acted as though all was well. He acted like nothing had changed.

He had changed. He was no longer perfect.

He found that he could sympathize with the cruel—with the human traffickers, the abusers, the violent, the squalid and sordid—as never before. They were all just humans, trying to find their way in the world, doing it badly. Surely at some point each of them had discovered that they were imperfect. Where did one go from there? The news on television, in the papers, made him sick, but not because of how bad the news was. The news was always bad. The talk last night between his uncles about the Latimer case had reminded him of that. The father's impossible choice to put an end to what he felt was his daughter's suffering.

The news made him sick because of the condemning voices that rained down on anyone who misstepped. There was such hatred and damnation in those condemnations—such blithe unawareness that they could be the next to fall.

He would not misstep. Not again. Not out loud. He ran harder. His stride was fleeter, more powerful than ever. He felt compassion for every person on death row in the United States, on lifetime sentences in Canada, for everyone whose livelihood was shattered by a moment out of line, by a mistake once made and never forgotten.

What about a mistake twice made? Was there such a thing?

He had to rest. His stride slowed. He was wrong. He was in the wrong. He could admit it to himself. He could say, aloud, that he wasn't proud of himself. He could say that he had learned, that he would be different.

He was no longer perfect.

He breathed. He sighed.

Perhaps no longer being perfect was, in fact, an important recognition. Something that happens as we grow up.

But he couldn't be sure. It hurt like hell.

Last night he had had a dream that left him fearful, afraid, running. It was, it had to be, an effect of his course last semester on the Second World War. It was unoriginal, but terrifying nonetheless. It was one of those moments in which clichés come alive.

In the dream, he was an S.S. Commander, working in a concentration camp. He had looked down and seen his uniform once he realized what he was doing. Buchenwald, Dachau, Auschwitz. He was pulling corpses from the gas chamber. The tiles in the chamber were white, but were gritty and chipped. He saw the fateful grates. What shocked him, more than anything, was the human scale. The gas chamber was small. It was cramped and underground. It was proximate, it was close.

He was pulling on the bodies of the dead, going over them for anything of value. He knew, he had learned in class, that the bodies would be naked, that those murdered were told to leave their belongings behind as they went into the chambers, but in his dream they were clothed. They had had valuables upon them. Working from behind a gas mask, his vision had fogged up more and more with each watch or ring that he found until he could see only through a thick haze.

An image fixed in his mind of a dark-haired woman rolling toward him when he pulled. He had taken the glasses from her unmoving face, her dead eyes that could no longer use them. He had wiped froth from her mouth, let her hair cover blood from her ears. She was human, all too human.

Awake now, John remembered the film of the bulldozers, remembered the horrid images, the shoes piled up. The stacks of things unrecountable.

How could one be happy, be whole, once one learned of the Holocaust, the Shoah? There could be no poetry after Auschwitz. He felt that he had learned, learned at a gut level, understood that he, too, had the same capacity to hurt, the same capacity to kill.

How could he be whole again now that he held this cruel knowledge? How should people continue to be in the world, once they recognize that they are connected to all of this horror? Humans were, are, barbaric. Poetry was, is, barbaric.

The dream was too easy, too. It was just a compilation of well-trodden images.

Yet it terrified him.

Of course, he would never have been whole anyhow. He was realizing that horrible truth in earnest now that he was an adult. Did it make him hard? Obdurate? Flinty? He knew that his behaviour around the others—his siblings and his cousins—could be domineering, his restraint seen as aloof. He did what he could. Some days he felt like he could not speak.

A leaf fell at his feet as he crunched up the drive. The house, the cabin, was quiet from this side, the truck and Jéanne's VW now both parked alongside his parents' Range Rover, his aunt and uncle's

Subaru. A leaf fell. Its colour had turned. He would never again be whole. A false phrase: it implied that he had been, once. Never.

Voices were in the air as he rounded the cabin. The voices were those of his siblings and his cousins. They were down at the water.

He would join them. Perhaps he could warn them somehow of what was to come. Could he do that? Would they listen if he broke the barrier that kept him from sincerity? They were too young. Perhaps this hurt that he felt was something that they each had to learn. Each in their own way.

He took off his shoes. Then he peeled off his socks. He began a short dash down the path, past his siblings and cousins playing in the muck—it looked as though they had been doing so for some time—and he entered the water wearing the rest of his running clothes. At least he could join them, commune against the time and the years to come. The water felt like a great sob as it pressed against his lungs.

*

Daphne read a line about becoming magical as her cousin plunged into the water next to her. A drop of water landed on her page. She watched John surface in the lake soon thereafter, a few metres from the dock. The sun was behind her, shining down on the lake—he was in the sun, shimmering. He began to swim a few strokes, then stopped, bobbed, floated along the surface, his hands moving, keeping his face above the water.

He always seemed so comfortable, Daphne thought, at home in his body, yet stern, restrained—sad even.

Daphne was the next oldest of the six of them. She did not feel at home in her body. She knew that she could be graceful, knew that she was slender and tall. She knew how boys and men responded to her. She understood what the novel she was reading was saying, as well as what it meant—yet she did not feel at home in her body. She wished that she could feel John's apparent ease, or her mother's, too, for that matter—her mother who seemed to rise above the petty squabbles, who was somehow not careworn or touched in the way that other mothers were. Her mother was like a crisp gingham tablecloth, yellow and blue.

Daphne looked over to the other children, who were piling muck up on the shore. Benjamin, Celeste, Michael, and Helen had made a good-sized mound of it by now. She could see that Celeste's interest was flagging: now she stepped a little bit further into the water, the shimmering blue reaching up above her knees, above her waist, up to her chest now—to her chin. And now Celeste floated there, twenty metres from shore.

So she floated: so she had left the other children there, still mucking about. The day was beautiful. The water was at its warmest at this time of the year. It was still bracing, but it would do wonderfully. Celeste's hair floated about her.

Well, let it, she thought, for it was wonderful hair. Let the other girls at school gripe, for she was still marvelous. Here she was, while the other children were still playing in the muck from the bottom of the lake. It was summer, after all, and all was well.

*

From inside, William saw the children there, at play, at rest: calm. His concerns weren't theirs. They could simply enjoy the day. He couldn't remember the last time that he could have done so. He couldn't remember the last time that he was bored. He always had in his mind some cares, some worries for the house or for the cabin or about some issue at work. Some minor errors that he might have made once, in the past, now distant, haunted him in the present. Things that lay there in the past might or could, he knew, one day find him again. Would they? Would a minor indiscretion a decade ago cost him his all today? Or even just a part of it? Were his worries ever founded? Was it best to plan for a worst-case scenario? Complicated he was not. He prided himself on being straightforward: he wished to keep that role in his household and in his life. Plan for catastrophe, live simply.

It seemed both remote and yet possible, William imagined. He imagined Clare's disappointment in him, in his inability to inhabit joy. Still, he was brave enough. For all of his faults, he was constant: he was as loyal as he could be. He did try his best: only sometimes his best fell short.

Ah, but we are all at fault, he thought. He traced a finger in the dust on the windowpane.

We are all imperfect. Perfection could not exist—even the thought held a tinge of fascism in it. Surely the good that he did now, for his children, for keeping them in the bright sunshine of this August day late in the millennium, recommended him somewhere.

Helen had been so glad, coming back from the dump, to head down to the water. She looked forward to reporting on the bears.

Simply put: he loved his children. He would do most anything for them.

Anything? He thought over the idea, and the word: anything. Any thing. He parsed it. Yes, he knew in his heart, absolutely anything. His children had changed him, he thought as he wiped away all of the dust from the casement with his finger, up the edges of the window, and then as he moved to the next windowpane.

But how, if he were to be exact, had his children changed him? He couldn't be certain. On the one hand, he loved them in a way that he couldn't describe. He had been there for the moment of each of their deliveries, there with Clare in the room every time. He remembered being handed each of his children after their respective births. It was a procession now in his memory, one birth after the other: John, Michael, Helen. They were so small, so vulnerable. He had then understood vulnerability for the first time. He knew with what ease they could be hurt. He knew how easy it would be to fuck it all up. Therein lay the terror of parenthood: therein lay his desire to do the best that he could, even if it would sometimes fall short of good enough.

On the other hand, fatherhood had made him hard in some respects, he knew. Rigid. Careful. Fathers seldom came off well in stories, after all. Think of Lear. Think of all of Canadian literature. They kill us for their sport: flies to wanton boys are we to the gods. He would not be a

Lear. Nor a panzer-man, a bastard. If he could help it. They fuck you up, your mum and dad. He had grown perhaps flinty, concerned— flighty, even. He worried that his over-careful steps might damage them, too, that he was too reserved. Yet the world seemed to call for such reserve these days, he thought. They may not mean to, but they do. Philip Larkin's poem flashed through his head. It was a lose-lose situation, when looked at from a certain angle.

Still, he didn't hurt anyone by being reserved. He didn't exactly triumph, either, but now, father that he was, his job was to cede the stage, piece by gentle piece.

Now my charms are all overthrown, and all that, William said.

Mackenzie, from across the room, harumphed and farted at the same time. Outside, the children played. It was, in essence, their job to take his place: it was up to them to depose him. Despise him, if necessary. Yet perhaps they could all do it cooperatively: with civility. They could work together toward the same goal.

*

That they could play for so long now, unsupervised, unaccompanied, and be trusted still to come in for food, to moderate their sun exposure, to avoid shitting their pants, more or less to take care of themselves—it was such a relief! thought Clare, who had also glanced out, one floor above William, to see how the kids were getting on.

She had just finished helping Jéanne and Françoise to unload the groceries. Clare was making herself a lunch, pouring her first glass of pinot gris for the day, planning to follow the sisters out to the deck, to join them in the summer sun to enjoy a meal, have a laugh, revel in the spark of three aging women who had known each other for years, among whom there were few surprises and many memories.

Mike and Doug walked into the kitchen: they were fixing supplies for another afternoon's canoe trip.

Clare thought deeper into her afternoon. She thought about trying to steal time to read her novel, about making another supper. It was amazing, in a sense, that another supper had to be made every single day! They were such creatures of familiarity, comfort, and habit.

The brothers grabbed beer from the fridge, went looking for bread, for chips, for apples. Basic things. They were arguing, although mildly, about David Milgaard. And then they turned to discuss what politicians and the media were terming free trade.

Then they were gone, leaving Clare still in the kitchen, still gathering her lunch, its more precise brie and olives and leftovers that were the right match for an early afternoon's sunshine.

She looked out the window again: the children were gone, had left somewhere. Even John, who had been in the lake, was nowhere to be seen. Daphne had taken her towel and her book. All traces were gone. Clare wondered how long she had been in the kitchen. She slid open the heavy glass door, pushing it with her shoulder when it stuck, and headed outside to the deck.

Jéanne and Françoise were already deep in discussion, again about the children.

Françoise really was very patient with them all, Clare thought. She thought again of her childless brother. John would never manage it so well!

Françoise loved being an aunt, an aunt with a slight tinge of scandal. She was wise, witty, attractive, and always well-dressed. She wore large black sunglasses now. An aging woman and an academic, she wore the aspect of someone beautiful who had had her lovers when she lived in Paris—some of whom were now quite famous, though she would never divulge—and who tolerated working at her prairie university because it allowed her to spend portions of the year abroad on research. Clare knew that of course it was much less romantic than that—she knew that being single at Françoise's age had consequences, and she knew that the university was a bureaucratic juggernaut. She knew that Françoise's closest confidante was her therapist. But, still, Françoise bore it all very well. Also, her body had never carried babies: her breasts remained more or less in place, and her abdomen was still taut. She worked at it, one could tell, but Clare felt the weight of her life in comparison.

The children had left and gone somewhere to play.

Daphne reads so much now, Jéanne was saying. She always has her nose in a book. I think that she imagines we don't know what she is reading, but of course we always do. We keep putting the books there for her to find, after all. I suspect she would be scandalized if she knew that we knew what they were about. Isn't that odd! Do you remember thinking, as a teen, that our parents mustn't—couldn't—have known the salacious things that we dreamed of and did? That there was no possible way for them to have known? That we were the first to invent everything—sex first and foremost? Such a funny time.

I wonder if you might provide something suitable in French for her next birthday, Jéanne continued after a brief pause, addressing Françoise even while welcoming Clare into the conversation. For the children were all in French schooling, after all. Hugo? Camus? Colette? Anaïs Nin? What should she be reading by now?

All of the imponderables of what it may be that leads to a life that one may love. That one may look at and feel, ah, that's just it. Like a hat perched on one's head at just the right angle. The conversation continued: the wine glasses were filled. It was pushing toward two o'clock.

In the city there would be clocks around us, Clare thought. She should turn soon to thinking about cooking dinner. The roast, it wanted doing. At least tomorrow the plan was for a barbeque, for hamburgers, for William and his brothers to burn something on the rusty, propane-fuelled grill on the deck. Their moments of fitting in with expected Albertan rusticities.

And Benjamin! Françoise added, shifting the subject. He seems to be doing so well now.

Yes, said Jéanne, it's true.

They had been concerned about his schooling. Benjamin was a younger child, after all, and the middle child. He hadn't seemed to show as much innate aptitude as his older sister. He had become discouraged, anxious, worried. But he was getting along now, with sports and math keeping him on track. The change had come as a welcome surprise.

Clare added her voice, comparing Michael, also her middle child, after all, surly and teenaged. Yet he would do well in the end. She could at least state her confidence in that much. She could!

Yet how she worried after all of her children! Was John too serious? Michael too grouchy? And Helen: was she paying enough attention? She was often dreaming. Too often? There was always something about which to be concerned.

*

When Clare's glass emptied, she used it as a pretext to retire to the kitchen. It was time to begin preparations. She could come back out soon. The roast wouldn't roast itself. She went back in the sliding door. It was a bit sticky. It ground along unhappily in its frame. It would want tending to: she must ask William.

From inside, she could still see Jéanne and Françoise out the kitchen window. How glamorous and tranquil they looked from here! And William, it turned out, was in the kitchen already. He was peeling potatoes.

I thought that we wanted these for supper, he said.

Clare was so pleased to see him! No one else was about: Françoise and Jéanne were on the deck; Mike and Doug were in the canoe; the children were God knows where; and of course her brother John hadn't come after all. Clare loved William in this moment for knowing what she needed. She could have cried. She felt a momentary welling up in her chest and then took a deep breath, a yogic breath through the nose, bringing her spirit back to earth like a tethered balloon. How perfect William was, after all!

They set to work.

The carrots want peeling, too, William said.

The roast needs to go into the oven right away, Clare responded.

Yet for the most part they worked in silence. William knew when to hand her the bulb of garlic: Clare knew when to take a light step out of the way of the fridge door. He knew to boil the kettle: she knew to pass him the butter dish. So time passed: so the building of the supper progressed. Soon Clare was putting the roast into the warmed oven, and soon William was setting down his knife on the cutting board, a pile of leafy detritus to one side, the meal's accompanying dishes on the other: a salad, a large pot of potatoes ready to boil, a fridge resplendent with garnishes and heaps of food to feed them well into the evening's card games, into the next bottle of wine, and into the next bright dawn.

Silly thing to do, roasting on a hot day like this, William offered.

Clare shrugged. So it goes. If they had a larger barbeque they could do it outside.

Clare wondered where the children had gotten to: William asked where the kids were.

I'll go and see downstairs, said Clare. She headed out of the kitchen.

William did the same, except that he headed toward the couch with his book, destined for a nap. Some light cabin book—its cover flashed in his hand.

At least he is a reader, the thought again ran through Clare's mind, dissatisfied for a moment. His need for attention could grate on her when she had not the time or patience for it. His too-quiet reflection on the world took up space. Yet, at those moments, he was perfect, too! She frowned at herself.

He was off, then, to the living room, a room that was swaddled in sunlight from all sides, in all seasons. It was a room in which napping seemed inevitable.

Clare took the other tack, headed toward the stairs. The stairs were one of the few ill-lit parts of the top floor of the cabin, cut off from the light by the bedrooms on the east side of the building and by the kitchen on the west. The white walls held her in a dull fix of air, air, air, and a darkening descent to the level below.

Downstairs was darker. Even though the west side of the cabin was flanked with glass, with a doorway that led to the lake, it was darker. The deck above shaded these windows, windows that looked out into the trees, the mature spruce and aspens that lined the path toward the shore, the beach, the water, the boathouse, the dock—toward the outdoors, toward life in the sun, the life that her children both lived and shunned in alternate measures.

And where were the children now? They weren't downstairs, either.

Clare walked to the television room under the stairs, a dark, enclosed space that served well for the screen but for little else. The couches were rumpled: blankets were strewn. But the children weren't there.

Clare returned to the main space, headed toward the door. The children had been through not long ago, she could tell. There was a warmth: there was a glow of childhood nearby. She saw the mess at the door. The mud! The children had tracked in mud from the lake, from the path. It clung to the mat at the door. It spread onto the cool linoleum tile of the floor. Slap, slap, went feet in Clare's mind. The mud was wet.

How like when they were very young! Clare thought.

The prints were larger, however. She would have to clean it up. Not yet, however, she reminded herself. No, first she must let the mud dry, its great clumps. Then she could sweep: she could vacuum. The mud must be allowed to air, allowed to dry before it could be cleaned.

How like the children! Clare thought. How like life! The quiet that we keep so that our lives might continue in peace. Only once the past has dried, desiccated, and departed might we get down on our hands and knees and dust it up.

Corridor

Time rolled. Time twisted and turned, as it does. The world changed: the world stayed the same. John's career was going to be a success after all, Clare and William sighed, now that he had graduated into the officers' ranks. It had taken them time, but they were able to appreciate some of the structure that he sought. Investments flew, and grew, while the world around them celebrated the end of history. But technology—robots—wouldn't save them all. Benjamin had had to concede that point. Investments went bust as the decade wore on. Seattle and San Francisco were at a standstill, but that, at least, was still preferable to life outside of the West, Doug maintained. Jéanne agreed: she had travelled for herself to see, after the divorce. The settlement had allowed her to go, and Mike kept the children, now so much closer to adulthood. The children seemed to grow visibly overnight. The year ticked over and over again: the millennium came and went without so much as a hiccup. They did not all spend New Year's together: they spent it with friends, with colleagues, with lovers. John took his girlfriend at the time to New York. Jéanne had been in Paris. William and Clare stayed in Calgary, waiting up for Michael and Helen, who were each with friends of their own. Mike rang it in alone. Doug was travelling: somewhere, some conference. Françoise was at home, between the semesters. Clare did not know what her brother did on that night, but he had come for Christmas, at least. The clock ticked over: they raised their glasses: the new millennium began. Summer came, went, came. One morning, the dog died.

2.

Clare wondered what to think of this summer, what to think of the wind-lashed shores of the lake. The leaves were yellowing, she thought, a little bit sooner than they usually did. Pay it no mind, pay it no mind! It was the rhythm of the year.

And John wouldn't come again! Her dear lost brother. But he had come to the cabin, what was it, two years ago? But it had only been for a weekend, and he had made William pick him up in Red Deer— John had caught a ride that far with a friend, someone whom Clare didn't know. Neither did she know her younger brother any longer. Perhaps she could not know him after all. It was not that she hadn't tried: she had. Yet it was his life to live, and she would give him the space to do so. He had chosen a different route, one apart from the family of his birth. It was not malicious: it just was.

Yet she wondered. If he were here, would he enjoy the wind off the lake this morning? What wasn't to like! The leaves were rustling outside. Clare could hear the sound through the open kitchen window. It would be hot again in the afternoon.

Yesterday they had all been sticky, damp with sweat. It had clung to them, dampened their shirts. Even John—her dear son and brother's namesake!—had shortened his run, gone earlier than usual in the morning. Everyone had spent a part of the day in the basement where it was cooler.

Now this morning it was the wind! It would die down—Clare was sure of that—but you could see the leaves turning. There had been a chill overnight after all of the heat. Summer was so short.

It felt like just yesterday that they had been shovelling out in Calgary, out from under all of that late snow. Now here summer was, ending. It was ending and it was still mid-August.

Clare looked up, looked out of the window. It would be fine today, she thought. She would go down to the lake. The lake was inviting her to read, to swim.

Perhaps she would ask the children to cook. Jéanne would not come—she and Mike still would not be in the same room together, so it was small surprise—so Clare could not rely on her steady hand. Perhaps in a few years' time, she hoped, Jéanne and Mike could share space again. For the children's sake, if nothing else.

The change had so affected the children: Daphne was further into her books than ever; Benjamin was sullen; and Celeste—well, Celeste was realizing that she had a body, and one in which young men were, indeed, very interested.

Mike had been looking rather frayed, too: he had sole charge of the children for the week up here and well beyond. Jéanne was in Paris right now, headed next for Prague.

Even so, even with their closeness, Clare did not know quite what had driven the two apart, even now, as the dust settled. As the mud caked. It hadn't, it seemed, been the usual divides after all: money, infidelity, that sort of thing. It had just transpired. And now Jéanne was travelling! Oh, it was good to see her doing that, anyhow. Clare looked forward to hearing about her travels, even though they weren't in quite as much contact these days. She would have to make a point of inviting Jéanne to bring the children down for a visit when they were back in the city, she told herself.

In the meantime, however, at least Françoise had come. For Clare would otherwise be without another woman of her generation. She would be fine with the three brothers, William, Mike, and Doug, and the children, but it was so much better to have Françoise there too. She had come without her sister, no less, even though she had been freed of obligations to the family as a result of Jéanne and Mike's divorce!

Clare knew how Françoise admired—and was admired by—her nieces and nephews, by all of the children, how she was part of the family, even with the bonds that had brought her into it severed. She was, indeed, a part of life here. For Clare, Françoise was a tremendous consolation. Family was thicker than blood, Clare might say. It was not just blood: it was something much greater.

Now here she was. Françoise was making a salad in the kitchen even now, a tasteful coffee standing on the counter beside her. She was getting ahead of food-making for the day. And how well she looked! Clare thought: she was aging nicely, her refinements accentuated by the hair that she was allowing to grow in in grey. Françoise wore a light scarf—not at all necessary on a day like today—that was a perfect complement to her outfit. She was worldly, well-travelled, and dishevelled—but in an artistic manner than highlighted her strengths.

And she chopped a cucumber with such decisiveness, too.

Clare came into the kitchen to join her. Françoise was happy to have the company: it vitalized her. For Françoise had come to the cabin out of devotion to Clare. In every other respect, to be here without her sister did feel awkward. Yet Clare held the world up and together, without ever seeming to realize that she was doing so. She did not know her own beauty, her attractiveness, her cunning, or her wit, Françoise thought. She was as genuine as could be. Clare would do as well in Paris, France, as in Paris, Ontario—in Marrakesh or Madrid, too, for that matter. She held the world up, never realizing everything that she did to make it so. It was devastating: it was beautiful.

Françoise could compare her with others whom she had known: friends, lovers, colleagues, acquaintances. Clare managed to achieve so much between them all without ever having to say or do anything explicit to make it happen. Her accomplishments didn't need listing on the page or announcing from a lectern. Rather, she put meals together, she saw to suitable social groupings, she was kind—even to the point of self-effacing—and she seemed to know what other people needed. She also knew how the best and most correct circumstance could be assembled without ever making it seem artificial or put upon. Françoise loved that.

For Françoise had been to too many academic events that were so staged, so phony: so many dinners with people who were hostile beneath their polite veneers, whose civility was marred by the social arrangements. She remembered an unfortunate dinner in Austria, another in Italy. A sherry reception at a university in northern England that just went on and on forever, everyone gritting their teeth and keeping a stiff upper lip. Granted, the cabin was not the desultory academy, with its petty jealousies and ill-concealed hatreds, but Clare managed just as well in the city, in social situations in which bankers like William somehow mixed with anti-capitalist artists or social services run by socialists. Somehow, Clare could find the right canapé to bridge the conversation. She might fret about it, yet she would always bring it off. It was why the cabin was so comfortable, in Françoise's estimation.

Françoise knew that she had her own charms, but these charms were much more based on detachment—and a detachment based, at least in part, on fear. It is easy to be well-dressed, beautiful, and quiet while swirling one's Syrah or sipping one's sherry, provided that one had access to that sort of thing. She listened well and held an allure over others as a result. Yet she seldom acted first, and was, at the end of the day, still afraid of being discovered to be less smart, less desirable, less interesting than others believed. Past lovers had seen this fear because, like anyone else, at day's end she had a mortal body. Yet she hid it well. Now only her closest friends and her therapist knew of her terror. It was, for her, a lurking dread.

Clare picked a hair from her own clothing—one of Mackenzie's. Françoise noted how Clare did it with an easy grace.

Clare had cleaned since Mackenzie's passing, of course. It had been an embolism, the thing that had led to William's dog's death. It had indeed been tragic, but also merciful in its brevity. Since then she had cleaned the cabin several times over. And the cleaner whom she had out once every year, at the beginning of the season, had left the cabin all but spotless. She was a cleaner from nearby who could understand little of the Briscoes and MacDougalls but their money.

Yet it was Mackenzie's hair on her elbow—no, on her forearm, really.

William's dog. He was out now, William was, tramping about the property, the sort of walk that he would always have done with the dog in the past. Clare knew the sound of the two of them crunching through last year's leaves in the undergrowth. She missed Mackenzie, too, though she was pleased not to have to clean up the everyday canine messes.

But William, William was ill at heart with his loss: his daily companion was gone, his quiet was more complete: his interlocutor had left him. Clare saw all of that, knew it, sympathized with it— even while she wished, in some sense, that she could have brought that same sort of solace to William all along.

How hard the children had taken it, too! Yet they were of an age, Clare thought, at which it could simply have been one of life's changes. She had not expected them to be so upset over the dog. For Helen, just eighteen, it was hardest, for she looked up most to her father and had spent many walks with Mackenzie. Helen was red in the eyes for days after Mackenzie passed, and led the family in their makeshift funeral.

Funny, though: Clare had not thought much of these things during the past few months, perhaps because they had not been at the cabin— except for very short bursts of visiting early in the summer. Now, being at the cabin for an extended stay brought out her thoughts. Mackenzie had died, after all, back in the fall. It had been some time ago. Yet there was something about William walking alone through the trees—or perhaps with Helen—that prompted her to think of Mackenzie. She thought of the patterns that we grow into, the patterns that we leave behind, whether we are ready to do so or not.

*

For William was, just now, walking in the trees, alone. He wondered if he should get the canoe out, perhaps even dust off his fishing tackle. He didn't have a license to catch fish, he remembered. He debated with himself, wondered if he cared. He could get a license in town, of course.

But perhaps just a trip in the canoe: something different. He should invite Mike—that is, if he decided to go. Mike had been through a difficult time, even if he had brought it on himself. Mike still looked rough, two years now after the separation and, later, the divorce.

Ah, but the course of life is seldom straightforward, after all. And it would be sad if it were just a straight line between the cradle and the grave.

William touched the bough of a tree. At least, for him, these days he could work on making his corner of the world a better place, whatever his faults may be. Ultimately, he knew, his faults were minor ones, ones of lack and small failure. He stepped over a downed log.

These walks had been nicer with Mackenzie. The dog would bound off the path that the two of them had worn through the bushes, on top of what William supposed had been a path worn by ancient deer. Then Mackenzie would come back: then he would race off again.

In secret, and just to himself, William was proud of the trail that wound around the perimeter of the land. His tread kept it there: it marked his passage. Mackenzie would come back covered in undergrowth, twigs, seeds, sticks, all stuck in his fur. William only brushed him at the end of their stays: there really was no point until then of doing so.

Sometimes Mackenzie would bring things to William: a stick, some grass, a piece of garbage, and, one memorable time, a toad. The toad had just sat there on the path when Mackenzie tenderly set it down. William had nudged it, and off it leapt. Mackenzie did not fetch. All of the things that he brought were curiosities for William.

Companion species, William had heard them called, dogs, cats, and beyond, but even that term seemed to imply his precedence over the dog. Who was companion to whom?

Trunkless legs of stone, William muttered under his breath.

What remains? What was the difference between William's passing and his dog's? What traces could he leave? Should he leave? After the end, the rest is silence. William pictured nothingness as best he could, an exercise that he had done since he was six, alone and frightened in his bed, his parents, below, taking care of the quotidian, taking care of his two little brothers. He could summon up a vision of nothingness, of non-being, with as much ease as Sartre, he reckoned. He was good at it. He had slept poorly as a child.

William's nothingness was absolute: it was a distended space that had no concrete shape, and into which he saw himself falling—or, rather, which engulfed him. It consumed him whole. He remembered watching the film adaptation of *The Neverending Story* with his children in a cinema, years ago, and seeing some version of his nothingness rendered in celluloid on the screen. It was the wolf that had scared his children, but it was the Nothing that got to him. The film had terrified him.

So, then—what can matter? William thought. That old cinema was still there, on Eighth Avenue, but it was decrepit now. Its days seemed numbered. Even the bank seemed distant from out here.

William had grown more distant at work, too. Precise, correct, but distant. He had grown meticulous and scrupulous. His dog mattered more than every transaction put together, every stock rise or dip. He had grown to feel Zen about it: in fact, he had begun to read about Zen, and his work had become more of a means to an end, an end with the meaning of doing as well as he could with his children, of engaging in what charitable acts he could in his life.

Nothing could mean more than his dog. He walked through the bushes, looking for things that Mackenzie would have liked. Should he get another dog? Something smaller, more city-worthy? Worthy of the retirement that was beginning to come into view? But Mackenzie's time had been special: it had been the time of his children's youth. He had been the dog with whom they had all grown up, the dog who had protected—nay, herded—his young brood. Mackenzie had been the dog who huddled up with Helen on blustery nights, the dog who had tolerated everything that they had managed to throw at him.

Though he never did fetch.

And now the children were no longer keen on pets, nor were the boys at home.

John was in the officers' ranks, so alien to William—yet he seemed to be successful. Michael had gone to Queen's, had excelled at history, and was now on his way in a few weeks to England—off to drippy, sleepy old England, which William still loved, all these years later. Michael would go to Nottingham, pursue a master's degree on a partial scholarship, see where his path might lead him. His girlfriend would not be going, but it was, Michael said, to be an amicable parting: she was off to graduate school at Columbia: they had their separate trajectories ahead of them. And young Helen was going to be leaving, too, and soon, off to start her university studies at McGill, in Montréal. All far from home, but present for now.

William walked through the brush with a feeling of some alarm, imagining his youngest living in Montréal, living in a narrow apartment off St-Laurent with several friends, as she was planning to do. He and Clare would be childless, as well as petless, in a few weeks. Had he not been waiting, part of him, for years for this moment, for its freedom?

Yet all that he felt was sorrow: the sorrow of his aging body, the accumulation of mistakes and missteps, every moment that could have been perfect. The children had grown, and now he got up in the night neither to calm a crying child nor to upbraid a wayward teen, but because of habit. Habit and an enlarged prostate. He could weep. But he would not, not here.

He wished—how ardently he wished—that he could convey the years ahead to the children, that he could spare them the heartaches and losses that the early false starts of adulthood were only too likely— were already beginning—to bring them.

He flipped a log with his boot and watched wood bugs scurry for cover.

*

The children, the children, too, missed Mackenzie, even if they wouldn't be interested in a new dog or a dog of their own. Something had been missing since their dog's passing.

John knew that a pet was not the right thing for him, not soon. His life was both too regimented and too uncertain for anything like that at this stage. Perhaps later. In a few days, he would be back at Petawawa and then onto who knows where. Michael, too, lived in uncertainty, with a plane ticket for Heathrow on September 23rd and a future that he couldn't predict. And Helen, well, Helen was just leaving home and did not think to ask such questions just yet.

Even their cousins missed Mackenzie: Mackenzie, the dog who had accompanied them on their summer romps around their aunt and uncle's cabin. Daphne, Benjamin, and Celeste had loved Mackenzie as their own, never having had a dog, their parents never wishing to have one. Daphne, for her part, imagined that a dog would have been one more complexity to her parents' divorce—she was happy that there hadn't been a family hound. Benjamin had left school directly into a post in a bank office in suburban St. Albert. He studied at night and on weekends so that he would be able to climb up the ladder at work. He was entering his own world but hadn't arrived there yet, much though he enjoyed other people's settled lives and pets. It was sixteen-year-old Celeste who most among them missed the shaggy presence of the old dog on this visit to the cabin, though—she was the one who most wished for a dog to be there still, or to have a dog of her own.

This summer's was a visit that, if anything, seemed to presage an end to their childhoods, or what was left of that time. An unspoken awareness of this shift seemed to be in the air. The absence of the dog signalled this change to Celeste. Or perhaps it was just an end to their innocence, Celeste reasoned.

The mood was somehow cloudy and grey, in spite of the August heat and humidity. The evening card games felt just a little bit listless.

*

Michael was in the bathtub upstairs. There was a shower downstairs, too. But the tub was large and, in the afternoons, unoccupied. People tended toward the cooler basement in the heat, if not into the blaze of the outdoors.

Michael could hear the crickets outside, chirping their loudest August chirrups. He would disappear under the water, he would.

The tub was large. He slid his feet up, out of the tub, and slid himself down, his back on the tub's bottom. He would come out clean, he knew that he would—he would be renewed—he would be ready to move to a new country, though perhaps England wasn't far enough, or new enough either.

Michael put his head back, his ears underwater, then his face. Just his nose stuck out of the water. He listened. The crickets had stopped, or else weren't audible. He breathed: he sighed. He could stay like this for hours.

He heard the odd bump around the cabin—perhaps the kitchen—no, the stairs. His siblings, or his cousins—parents, aunts, or uncles.

His hair floated, brown curls loosened. He would be renewed. He would be ready to read the past, to create change on and into the future. He would let the water out, and it would flow. He did: he pulled the plug.

The water swirled at Michael's head. The level began to drop. He felt it dropping. The water slid off his body, and he began anew. First he could breathe with more ease. The weight lifted from his brow. He returned to the air: he had to bear the full effect of gravity once more. As the water receded down his head, the drops fell from his ears, from his chest. He was clean. The water pooled: the hollow of his neck, the ducts of his eyes. On his eyes like tears, like Phoenician coins. He sat up, ready.

*

One day, you will be good for the last time.

One day, you will be bad for the last time.

One day, you will be virtuous for the last time.

One day, you will be tempted by evil for the last time.

One day, you will be alive for the last time.

One day, you will live the good life for the last time.

One day, you will work for the last time.

One day, you will play for the last time.

One day, you will have fun for the last time.

One day, you will be bored for the last time.

One day, you will be boring for the last time.

One day, you will have sex for the last time.

One day, you will love for the last time.

One day, you will hate for the last time.

One day, you will eat for the last time.

One day, you will drink for the last time.

One day, you will shit for the last time.

One day, you will piss for the last time.

One day, you will sleep for the last time.

One day, you will pay for the last time.

One day, you will fear death for the last time.

*

Doug thought all of these things as he lay in a chair on the deck in the heat. It felt as though he thought them all at once. He imagined nothingness.

Mike came onto the deck in order to join Doug. He shook a cigarette out of the carton and lit it. He leaned over the railing, looked down at the forest floor below and into the gloom of the lower level beneath him. He then raised his gaze and looked toward the water.

In the past, Mike would have expected the children to be down there. Instead, they were he knew not where. He was happy, though, with the reprieve. He exhaled, smoke coming back out through his nostrils and wisping into the air, like the waking of a magical dragon.

Mike looked over at Doug: his brother was sitting in one of the deck chairs, hat on his head, book set down beside him: something about Freud. Doug, he saw now, was looking at him, too.

So, Doug started. How fucked are we with another George Bush at the helm?

Mike smiled and took the bait.

Utterly, he said.

It was still the early days of the presidency, but anyone on the thinking left or centre, Mike felt, if not on the right, too, could see that this was going to be an ugly time.

What would Freud say, he added, indicating Doug's book.

It feels like we're in some sort of a dreamscape, Doug said, reflecting. On the one hand, we wonder how we could have ended up where we are. On the other, everything seems like it makes perfect sense, as long as the dream persists. One day we will all wake up, and then, I think, everything from this time will seem strange indeed. I keep thinking about the U.S. desert, about the south-central U.S., with its cacti and Wile E. Coyote and its long history of violence and colonization. As though the popularly imagined version of that part of the country has taken over all reason and sense. Freud would probably say something about a Daddy complex, though.

The conversation opened up: it was not so much an argument, today, as it was a series of agreements. The two brothers were, for a change of pace, in more or less perfect accord with one another. They shared grave concerns, the same grave concerns, for the future. Mike unwound into the details, the election's controversies, and into speculations about what would come next: retrenchment, in his view. He lit another cigarette. Doug tended toward introspection and the abstract. Yet they were speaking of the same thing after all.

Both brothers knew that the conversation was a way to talk about Mike's divorce without talking about it: being able to engage with the issues of the day—to be able to nuance the fine points through the verbal exchange of details in the news—was a means of confirming for each other that everything was all right. Mike was, in essence, confirming to his brother that, in spite of it all, he would survive, and that life would continue. Doug, in turn, was demonstrating that, whatever had happened, and whatever happened in the future, he viewed his role as one of supporting his brother. The news was a way of reminding themselves that there were greater forces at work, that their lives were microcosmic fractions of a much larger context, an unfathomable and vast existence through which they were flitting.

Doug was looking into the sky. A wisp of cirrus passed in a high summer meander. Perhaps it might cloud up later on.

Mike, finishing his cigarette, came and sat in one of the adjacent chairs.

The talk turned to Canadian politics, to the chances for the revamped Conservative party, which neither would vote for, but in which they maintained an intellectual and political interest.

Mike looked skyward as well: the sky was so shockingly blue. It seemed as though the more directly overhead one looked, the bluer it became. Was it perfectly blue? He thought of the artist Yves Klein, his particular shade of blue. Then he was reminded of a series of images that he had seen once—was it with Doug, somewhere? Something at a university—a series of images of a window created by a visual poet and an artist working together, each day's shade of blue a little bit bluer than the last.

Mike wondered if there was a way to look straight up—to look exactly, one-hundred percent perpendicular to the earth—and, in so doing, to discover the essence of what the colour blue was. Did it vary? The weather varied. Looking up, it seemed as though there was always a bit more blue, something, some hue, just a little bit deeper, whenever he let his gaze slip a fraction of a degree from the centre of his vision. Maybe that was it, then? The point of pure blue was an ever-deepening one, the point of absolute perpendicularity something that we tumbled into, not something that we could calculate with mathematical clarity.

The mechanics of blue were unfathomable. We fell, we fell into those points just at the edge of our vision—they were bottomless and pure—unreachable and dangerous. Just one search, unending, asymptotic.

Below them, behind the cabin, Mike and Doug heard the rumbling of the truck as it started up.

Time for the mid-point cleanup, Mike said.

Doug chortled in agreement. He returned to enjoying the sunlight, the view of the lake: the simple pleasure of still, for the moment, being.

*

Celeste was keen to see the dump—Helen had asked her to come along. William was happy to oblige. Although her joining did upset the father-daughter time that William and Helen shared on these jaunts, he was pleased to see the two girls' bond surviving their teenage years. Celeste sat in the middle of the bench seat, bumping along on the uneven road. She had imagined the dump in a certain way for a long time—she was hoping for bears.

The sunny day, with its clearing skies, the wind having died down, provided little more than a skiff of a breeze. They drove with the windows down, not saying much to one another. William drove along at his regular, even speed, unbuttoning his mackinaw in the warmth. His back was becoming damp against the seatback. His old T-shirt underneath welcomed the fresh air. He turned right, and then, a few minutes later, right again.

Soon, the rustling leaves gave way to the short gravel drive that led across the tracks and to the dump. They entered.

The dump was busier than Helen had seen it before: she thought of it as an almost private space, one that the dump supervisor shared with her and her father, the scavengers, and a few others on select occasions. Today all was abuzz: the bulldozer moved rubbish around—a flatbed was changing one dumpster of recyclables out for another, empty one—and a good eight or ten pickups roamed the middens (and the flies buzzed, too). They had added a fence around the edge of the dump, a flimsy divide between tree and trash.

Yet it was smaller than Celeste had expected: the heaps of garbage were seldom higher than a human's height, and you could see clean across the dump. The trees that bordered the cleared space were visible on all sides outside of the chain link fence.

This was it, then. Celeste could not but help feel the disappointment of a child who discovers that a mythical place is real, and that it is bounded by limits, edges. The dump was still exciting, but it was not quite the place that it had been in her imagination: dirty, dark, and a little bit dangerous. Its smell was unique, though, and Celeste could tell, now, what it was that happened with all of the stuff that she threw out. The truth was a bit prosaic, but it was nevertheless interesting.

They all clambered down from the cab of the truck. William stepped up into the box and began to throw bags. Helen and Celeste watched. Helen scanned the dump with interest.

I've never seen it this busy, Helen said. The bears will almost certainly stay away today. Though I'm sure they can manage the fences easy enough.

Oh! That's too bad, Celeste answered.

Inside, though, part of her was relieved. She had a curiosity to see the bears, but also—of course, she thought to herself—a fear of sharing close proximity with such powerful animals. She pulled her hair over her shoulder, away from the side of the truck against which she leaned.

Still, Helen said. Lots of birds today.

And so there were. Gulls soared overhead, a patchwork of them, circling the dump and squawking from on high. Every now and again they circled in low, landed in one corner or another of the mess. Ravens cawed in the trees. These swooped in along with the gulls, zoning in on any spots just vacated by the rubbish-tossing humans.

Were she further into the woods, Celeste imagined that she would hear jays, chickadees, and other birds, but the rumble of the bulldozer and the pickups muffled the sounds from beyond the dump. Yet the gulls and ravens were numerous. Their sharp cries punctuated the sounds coming from the engines.

Helen loved the birds, and, while she wondered and worried at what nourishment they were getting from the dump, she adored them. The sleek ravens, purple glinting from their feathers when the sun struck them just so. And the gulls, too: their loud cries, their migration. There was more than a single gull species about. She most admired the black-headed gulls, Bonaparte's, she had learned they were called. She imagined them soaring up to Labrador and Hudson's Bay before wheeling back south, passing through the human infestations that brought forth things like this dump.

And yet: what flowers could she find amidst all this evil? What blooms in the sweaty, stinky refuse? The birds did not seem upset— they did not care. If anything, they seemed overjoyed by the reek. Could they be? Helen did not know. She looked over the dump, made mental notes of what was there.

Celeste watched her cousin watching the birds and the land, and watched her uncle empty the box of the pickup. Helen appeared entranced. What was it in her, what registers could she feel and reach that Celeste could not?

For Celeste felt downright plain next to her cousin: her concerns seemed so humdrum, so everyday, that they could never be of interest to anyone—the opposite of Helen, who at this moment was enthralling to her. Celeste feared, from a very deep, dark place in her being, that the transparency of her own depths would be seen by others—would be revealed with as much ease as how the sun's rise dispels the darkness.

And yet Helen's rapture over the dump was a sight to behold: Celeste had to admire her cousin.

William finished the task. They all climbed back into the truck, trundled back through the dump. More trucks were arriving, scattering the gulls to the skies and the ravens to the trees. William paid, and they drove back up the gravel road.

Celeste noted the men working the dump, noted how the men driving the trucks tended to look just like the workers. Yet how can that be? she wondered. For she knew that the cabins in the area were all dear to purchase—to own—to maintain. Many of the owners came there from one of the two big cities. Was there some unspoken uniform for the dump about which all the men knew? Some secret code of masculinity that was inaccessible to her? The men who were coming, who were bringing down loads of trash from their lakeside cabins, were surely better dressed when they were at work in downtown Edmonton or Calgary. Yet here they all blended together, unshaven. It all seemed mysterious.

They drove along the route back to the cabin. William observed his daughter and his niece, each lost in her separate thoughts. He realized that it was a good moment, that nothing needed to be said, and that he should simply enjoy it. He also noted the paradox of recognizing that a moment was a good one, and, by recognizing it, no longer being a part of it, and therefore no longer being able to exist in its goodness.

Helen, for her part, thought of birds, about the mechanism of the beak, its opening and closing—of how ravens and crows stood, on hot days, with their beaks wide in order to let out the heat—of how birds like woodpeckers (which could sometimes be heard in the trees near the cabin) had beaks with a remarkable ability to perform so many tasks. She thought, too, of feathers: pinions, guiding feathers, tail feathers, down. How feathers responded to light, to wind, to water.

Celeste remained struck by the mysterious codes of male behaviour.

The countryside rushed past them all. The trees, the leaves, the cabins dotted the way under the heavy sun. The many driveways flickered in and out of the shadows cast by the trees that bordered them, each unique path up to each unique cabin—resulting in the most homogeneous of patchworks.

*

At the water's edge, Benjamin and Daphne were enjoying the summer's day. The others were working on tasks—simple chores of maintenance—or else relaxing elsewhere.

Benjamin and Daphne were allowing themselves to enjoy their break, their holiday time. Daphne was in the water: Benjamin was on the shore. The water was warm and calm.

It would grow choppy later on, Benjamin thought, out beyond their protected corner of the lake. For now, though, the water was still all the way across.

Daphne's swim was more of a drift, really—she was just allowing herself to move in the water, with slow, lazy kicks with her legs to propel her into the cooler depths offshore, near the dock. She had done her hair up and was even wearing goggles today. She had left her towel and book behind on the shore.

Daphne had reached the penultimate page of the text and was holding true to her new resolution—borrowed from somewhere that she had already forgotten—never to read the final page of any book. She found it a small tragedy, every time, for a story to end. Oh, there are endings—like the final ending, of course—but stories go on. Clarissa Dalloway's tale couldn't end, and neither could Jane Eyre's. Anne Shirley, mercifully, had many more books to inhabit, but that still didn't solve the problem. Daphne had decided to boycott endings and to embrace instead the open.

She rolled over onto her back and looked skyward, noting, too, how very blue the sky was today, although she couldn't be sure how much of that effect was caused by the slight tint of her goggles.

So she had set her book down, just before the last page. Some books were easier than others: some left key details until the last page. Most books, however, had already resolved their plots by that point. Nevertheless, she found a rebellious satisfaction in abandoning every book just before it ended, especially those from her studies.

Daphne let herself be pulled—pulled herself—in the green-blue water. The water held her, both within its embrace, and also, just, in the air. She bobbed at its surface. It was comfortable, comforting, to be held just at the point of ease.

Perhaps, afterward, that's what life might be, she thought.

Ashore, Benjamin had now drifted into a half sleep. He had been the last one up last night, had watched some silly film after he retired from the rest of the family. He was half-awake, too.

He allowed his mind to wander, first to an image that sometimes came behind his eyelids, fuzzy concentric circles that shrank into one another, pulsing in time to his heartbeat. The circles were brighter than usual, the sunshine seeping in through his closed lids. Good thing he had brought a hat, he thought. He could hide under the towel on which he rested his head, too, if he needed to do so. The circles pulsed, faded into one another. New ones came into view from beyond the periphery of his mind's eye.

Benjamin's mind drifted further, and now he could feel himself being held—he was being held with a firm, yet gentle grip, his torso, his abdomen, in a sure hold. He imagined looking out, looking down, and he saw that he was well above the ground now, seeing rolling fields, trees below. He could place the splashing in a small lake over which he floated. It was misty, but warm: straight ahead he could see clouds, low clouds, into which he was flying. He twitched, and the clouds began to dispel. It was overwhelming: it was tragic. It was, well. There was just no single way to put it. It was all hazy, too, unfocused, a series of concentric circles, drops falling one upon another in a pool of still water, in reverse, reflecting his face back up at him. If he only —

*

It was Helen who had the idea of the pageant.

For Mackenzie. Young Helen, headed to McGill University in a few days now. Clare could not believe that all of her children were grown, would be gone. Helen, little Helen, now leaving for Montréal, had concocted a pageant, a tribute, for Mackenzie. The details were to be a secret from the adults until the performance.

She had enlisted her cousins, who were enthusiastic, and her brothers, who had gotten past their embarrassment and had thrown themselves into the work of preparation with whole-hearted and unironic goodwill.

Helen was ready: Helen was a steady woman now, smiling, but just. Her hair had darkened. She had grown, then stopped, and was a smidgen taller than her mother. Her spirit had grown resolved after its earlier hesitations, and although she saw that the world around her was difficult, she felt that she would persevere. Her imagination was like a sad entertainer, down on his luck and in the heel, filling helium balloons in a snowstorm in the hopes of a crowd.

Helen was handy, too. She could build a rough and simple set for the show, provided that the others helped with puppets and costumes. She had chosen to take woodshop in school—a decision that had baffled her parents.

She had been working in the garage, the seldom-used building adjacent to the cabin. This space had picked up a great deal of scrap material over the years, like a junkyard couched in a small cavern. John had taken her on the short trip that had been necessary to find the rest of the things she needed. He had helped her with the selection and with the carrying. But the concept and the planning remained hers.

It was late in the summer now, as it always seemed to be. The mosquitoes had sallied forth and then died back. They were in retreat. Sometimes one could see a bat flittering at dusk.

Benjamin sat out in the evenings, picking something out on William's old guitar, which otherwise gathered dust from disuse. Helen was in the garage a great deal. The other children seemed, Clare thought, to be somehow absent, though they might often still be found at cards or else watching a film in the basement as the evening turned to night.

But not always.

The performance was to be the night before they decamped for the fall. Celeste had been working up the programs, writing precise script on pages in a broken, rustic style that evoked a lavish, Baroque decadence. She dated each program precisely: August 23rd, 2001. Though she had debated writing 23 August 2001. She preferred the superscript in 23rd. These letters allowed her a bit more flair.

Helen had been reading fin-de-siècle writers for the past couple of years, dipping in and out as the mood struck her. Baudelaire was perhaps her favourite, though of course he was rotten, too. And into the twentieth century, a mix of decades: Mallarmé, Anaïs Nin,

Colette. She loved the energy of decadent burnout, having never experienced its effects firsthand. Moths to a flame, her puppets would smoke (and smoulder). It was late in the planning when she solved that part, but she did. The boys were all impressed at how she managed it, too. She wanted the spectacle to be one that breathed life, even in death. Rimbaud. Hugo. Strindberg, Freud, Elliot, Pound, Woolf, Joyce, Stein, H.D.

Daphne, two years at McGill already completed, was struck as she revised the script—for the most part composed of stage instructions—that Helen had produced. It had the feel of Helen's reading, though none of the content, nothing repetitive or mimetic. She tidied transitions, suggested amendments. She did runs through the sections of the show with her cousins. She was struck.

The adults, over cards, sipped Chablis, rested, and were, for a moment, content. The fall would soon be upon them. Their thoughts turned toward September. Clare and William fretted in their own ways and by turns about being rendered childless, empty nested, though they were planning travel to ease their transition: they would go to Corsica.

Of all places! Clare thought. But it made its own sort of sense: William wanted to see where Napoleon was born.

Doug was entering his final year of working at the University of Alberta and would retire very soon. He was ready, he felt, in his bones and in his beard. It was time to make way before he outstayed his welcome, though he knew that in the opinion of some he had already done so.

Mike anticipated a fall with his children: Benjamin was living at home, though now working, commuting to the suburbs; Celeste was entering grade eleven. Mike and Jéanne grappled with the continued awkwardness of separation and time-share parenting.

Françoise anticipated a fall of fresh budget cuts to her university, or at least to her department, the constant harrying of institutional crises.

All of them, together, felt the weight of their years, hung onto each other for the support that they needed in order to see, to feel, that they were loved in spite of—or because of? One can never be too sure, Clare thought—the world outside of the cabin walls, the squabbles, the infighting: the adults who behaved in ways that were the opposite of what they tried to teach their children to be.

As glasses were sipped, as cards were dealt, as, one by one, they retired to read, to sleep, the softening light of the August days bore them along, and they were truer then than ever they might have been before or than they would be at any time after.

*

It was not until the next night, the last night of this stay at the cabin— well, almost the last, as Clare and William were staying one more night, to put things to rights, as Clare put it—that the children held the pageant.

The adults were ushered outdoors at sundown, a time that had started to come earlier as summer sped toward its conclusion. The day was still warm—not hot any longer, not full of glare, but warm—and the sun was setting. You could feel fall approaching: the leaves sounded different now whenever a stray breeze lifted them on their branches. And the first few leaves were on the ground, too, crumpled in beige and yellow heaps like lovers' discarded clothing. It was a beautiful day.

The adults had seen little of the children all day long, except in brief snippets. Mike, if pressed, would have to admit that he was a little bit drunk, having had his first beer at around 2 p.m. 14.00 hours. 14h00. With Doug. And then he had kept going.

It wouldn't get chilly yet, would it? wondered Clare.

None of them knew the extent of the children's plans: they had simply been invited outside—on formal, black-bordered invitations that were written on a sturdy stock. The programs, as they arrived, were pinned onto their chairs.

The chairs! William half-exclaimed. So that's where they were.

For here sat a selection of the dining room, basement, and deck chairs, carefully mismatched by Benjamin in order to set the tone, under Helen's strict guidance. There were eight chairs sitting there, facing the door to the garage. Two sets of four with a path between them.

The garage door was, for the moment, shrouded in a dark, heavy cloth. The children had fashioned the path from old holiday lights that Celeste had found in the basement storage. They gave off little light as the day fell, and yet their meaning was clear enough.

But why eight chairs? Françoise pondered. For they were only five, the adults were: Mike, Doug, William, and Clare, besides herself. Were others invited? Did they indicate the missing: Jéanne, perhaps Clare's brother John? Who else? Yet there were eight: eight chairs, a perfect assortment. Each with a program delicately affixed to the back.

Here lay a test for the five adults: how to arrange themselves? For they would need to occupy five out of eight seats, an odd arrangement, a clutch of eggs placed into an unusual carton. Clare led: she took a seat in the front. William sat next to her. Doug lounged into a seat behind them both in the back corner. A small aisle, the light-lined path, lay between the two sets of chairs. Françoise sat in the front, across the aisle from Clare. Mike sat behind her.

It's a better place for whispering, he leaned over to say in his ex-sister-in-law's ear.

The adult generation waited now, seated, facing the darkened garage. Some looked at the programs, but these offered little help. They were cryptically worded: a celebration in four acts, the programs promised, listing the children's names in age order. For M.

The sky was darkening to a deeper blue, with a hint of purple. Clare looked up and saw the first star of the night—or was it a planet? Venus? Mars? she wondered—overhead, over in the direction of the lake, which was quieter than usual today.

*

Then the pageant started. The shroud, curtain, dropped to the ground. Its heavy weight landed with a soft thud, its pile a generous rift of folds, crests, and valleys.

The adults were all stunned for a moment by the light—the white and yellow light that filled all that they could see. After a moment, as their eyes adjusted, they could see that it was an elaborately constructed set. Opening at the middle, it came to about waist height. The frontispiece was carefully worked, evoking a wasted decadence, old wood shining through gilded carvings of cherubs and vines.

It was a blasted scene from a long bygone era, Françoise thought.

Behind, a threadbare and torn curtain of deep maroon hung as a background, showing gaps into the workings behind, the ropes and riggings of an elaborate stage no longer much resembling the garage that should have been visible behind, William noticed. And where had they found all of this material? he wondered, before, entranced, he forgot himself in something that seemed to be otherworldly, like a butterfly losing the delicate powders of its wings, translucent yet airborne for the moment.

The show was something bigger, more encapsulating, than seemed possible.

The world is a sad and beautiful place—the thought flashed across Mike's mind as he looked up at what must have been Venus.

The pageant began with a procession: the six children, robed in black, their faces covered by monastic hoods, bore up the centre of the aisle, a small coffin on their shoulders. The brown coffin, brass-handled and flat-lidded, was covered with flowers—white lilies—and, on it, discernable to all, a large, golden M.

Aha! Clare clapped her hands, then quieted herself. Mackenzie! That's who the M was for. She looked around at the others, who were watching as well.

But what could it signify? William thought. He is gone: he is gone.

As the procession gained the stage, the pallbearers set the coffin on a small, raised dais that no one had noticed until this point.

The light was falling, Doug reasoned, which explained his failure to have observed such an obvious feature.

Then the black-hooded figures filed toward the set, breaking into two groups and parting, each heading into the wings—the garage, Clare reminded herself—and disappearing.

Then all was, for a moment, silence, until there was a snapping and a fizzling and then, all of a sudden, more light. A series of sparkling fireworks—flares? Mike wondered—sprung into life just ahead of the dais, flashing and sparking for a brief minute before descending, again framing and highlighting the set.

For now the set was being transformed: a new backdrop hung in place and Françoise could make out the image of a lake—their lake? It was clear, too, that the set was a stage in miniature, for here were puppets.

I didn't know that they could do that, Clare thought—but, then, aren't one's children always doing the most surprising things?

For there were many puppets emerging onto the stage, and from all directions. Perhaps twenty, William thought, but then that was impossible, as the children did not have hands enough to manipulate so many. And how finely, too, they were wrought! They seemed to be moulded from clay and painted, then dressed, or perhaps carved with the utmost care from a fine-grained wood. All of the adults were impressed, transported.

As the show began, many puppets filed or tumbled back offstage.

It was an historical recreation, Mike thought, as a canoe came into view with rough-looking men inside.

These new figures disembarked and met with several people who stood on the shore. One might expect it to be a moment of contact, of connection.

And so it seemed to be: the set changed. On the backdrop one could now see several cabins in the distance, smoke puffing cheerfully from their chimneys. A gruff man sat on the porch of one cabin and smoked a pipe. All of the smoke caught in the rafters of the set, then billowed out, up, and into the evening's growing collection of stars.

Clare hoped that it wouldn't set off the fire alarm. Was there one in the garage, she wondered?

(Helen had disconnected it.)

Along the trails, wagons were now to be seen, rumbling as they proceeded through the woods. A woman sat in one of these carts, a fretful expression on her face at each bump and twist in the trail. A small piece of china, as from a dollhouse, fell from the back of her wagon.

Men and women walked in and out of the forests, to the lakes, and back again. The initial puppets, the greeters on the shore, watched with concern. High in the set, an owl flew—that is, an owl rendered in puppet scale—across a waxing moon.

Clare did not quite like it when one of the men said—in fact it was written on a banner that unfurled and then disappeared—to one of the women that this country was too new for ghosts. But he was then run offstage by a series of spectres and shades, for it was too true: the denial of our ghosts and their eternal return, the haunting and the dread that put us all, one day, to rest. Because we are already ghosts.

But otherwise she was entranced.

Now the scene shifted again—a large banner descended to announce that it was the second act—and a series of men who looked like a scene from a photograph were gathered indoors, fussing over something that they couldn't quite seem to get right. Their top hats fell off, revealing balding pates. They were threadbare, bearded, and drunken. They smoked and, in silence, they swore.

The puppets moved about the stage, small dramas unfolding in each direction: some of them threatened each other, while others signalled with their hands to hush, to quiet, to make peace. Other puppets stumbled around, bumping into tables and the backdrop. Some wandered offstage and then reappeared. Even with the trappings all being made obvious, the workings of the set on full display, there was nevertheless a verisimilitude, a sense of liveness, that kept the events somehow whole, complete.

The scene threatened to descend into a brawl before, all at once, a loud, solitary bark brought them to rights. The puppets looked around at each other, in confusion, and there it was again: a loud, single bark from a good-sized dog.

Was it part of the show? Françoise wondered. Yet it must be, for otherwise why would the puppets have reacted so?

But the bark left more questions than it answered. The puppets now organized themselves and dusted off their beaver hats, arranging themselves into what, William realized, was the tableau of the signing of Confederation, the British North America Act. 1867 in Charlottetown. He breathed a sigh of recognition and relief.

In the background, a train hovered into view, it, too, puffing steam-smoke as the century drew to a close.

And, with that, a loud snap! sounded.

Or was it a clapping? Clare wondered.

At any rate, there was a snap, and the curtain was pulled to. The black drapery hid the stage as the intermission began. It hid the dais, the quiet coffin upon it. Clare noticed when the clap sounded—or the snap—how very quiet it was. And, indeed, it had been silent: the show was, in effect, a pantomime. All that the audience could hear was the raising and the lowering of pulleys, the gambolling of puppets upon the stage, the rustling of aspen leaves, and the lapping of the lake. It was as if each puppet wore a mask in turn, a silencing face-upon-a-face that hushed them into a mood of reverence, if not fear. It was like a somber enactment of something bigger, of a sadness that swept through the glancing corners of everyone's souls, sometimes glimpsed but seldom lingered over.

But now the intermission had been signalled and, Doug and Mike knew not whence, a table had appeared behind their seats, draped in black, and two black-hooded servers were pouring wine. Mozart's Requiem sounded in the trees—Mike looked around and found the speakers, hiding under the eaves of the garage.

The other children appeared, too, but from the house, all wearing their black robes. A loon sounded on the lake.

It was near dark now—the light was falling fast, even though the first half of the production couldn't have been much longer than half an hour. The table was lit with the same type of lights as those lighting the path toward the stage. Françoise looked to the trees just in time to see a bat gliding up into the twilight.

*

The five adults left their seats and sipped their wine in silence, a silence that was prompted by the descending night and by their shrouded servers.

But what could it all mean? Clare still wondered, mystified.

Everyone walked about; Doug went inside to use the bathroom. Françoise examined the trees, feeling their tactility in a way that she hadn't remembered doing before. Clare and William stood together, each occupied by their own thoughts. Mike had another glass of wine.

But then the lights flashed, and with the flashing the children disappeared. The third act was about to begin. Only the lights shining on the path and the stars overhead were visible. The adults sipped their wine and resumed their seats. Woollen blankets, shawls had been placed over the backs of the chairs.

How thoughtful! Clare thought, for the air was cooling.

Françoise draped her chair's blanket over her shoulders.

The third act was unlike the first two: one might have expected the historical pageant to continue, to open perhaps with Laurier declaring the twentieth century to belong to Canada. But the earlier mood was rent: noise and light blared to welcome the guests back to the pageant.

Oh—the wars of the twentieth century, Doug realized. So the show had not disrupted itself in its entirety.

Yet here was noise: here was light. Small fireworks went off, onstage: the backdrop was now a muddy canvas, torn and ripped. Across the stage, puppets were raging at each other. Some were marching for rights—suffrage, against fascism, for civil rights, access to abortion—for they held signs to indicate their demands—while others were at war with one another. Puppets fell where they stood. The cacophony was astounding, flashes punctuating everything. And beneath it all, now, a sound played, deep minor chords, slow and insistent.

Feeling as though the music was arriving from below, Françoise sensed that it held everything together somehow.

Of course, William thought: this is precisely what the last century would look like to people just coming into adulthood. What a misery we made of it, he harumphed, seeing Valencians running for a bomb shelter in the Spanish Civil War, and then a column of Nazis marching muddied puppets, who bore stars of David and pink and black triangles, off through barbed gates. What we must look like to our children.

But what was the import of it all? Clare kept asking herself. Why tell—retell—this period of time? What can we learn from it now? What can we learn from it here? Are we supposed to do so? She could not discern what was happening at first, as a heavy mist rolled forth and then resolved itself. A creaky model airplane, its propellers twisting, crossed the stage, its cargo bay opening. With its strings clear to all viewers, an enormous bomb rolled from the plane and descended.

Clever, Mike thought. But disturbing.

Now, drab, grey-clothed workers clumped in unison into a Gulag. A moment later, more U.S. planes came into sight and then attacked a Vietnamese jungle. The government of Chile was overthrown, mowed down. Revolutions stirred, and there was a loud roar from one knew not whence.

There was another tremendous flash, a boom as though it were a gunshot—or no, thunder, Françoise reckoned.

The scene went dark: and now it truly was dark, as the night had come on. Silence fell.

Doug placed his blanket on his lap to warm his thighs.

As their eyes readjusted, act four began (a banner told them). A small, yellow light came back on at the right-hand corner of the stage. A group of children huddled under a dirty grey blanket. They peeked out, their movements slow and deliberate. One by one, they pushed back the filthy covering and looked on the ruins of a century, cities blasted and forests levelled and babies murdered.

Then they caught sight of the dais, the coffin on it. One of them, a young woman, pointed—and the coffin began to lower.

But it can't lower there! William thought. He almost stood up, his hand raising in protest.

The coffin was just in front of the concrete pad on which the garage was built, after all. Yet lower it did. The children onstage, their faces lighted from below, watched, rapt, as smoke began to rise from the hole left behind by the lowering box. One of them, a young man, threw a clump of soil after it.

And then the smoke was general: it poured into the sky from the ground, then the stage, then from the garage in general. Behind the smoke, lights came on, flashing, strobing, and the noise of a million people rose, though each voice was indistinct.

But this time the mood seemed more resolved—almost joyful, Clare would have said.

The volume rose to a high level, then the lights flashed once more. The noise stopped, and the show was over. In the air, ashes and bits of paper burned, fizzled up into the night sky. They hung there among the trees, punctuation marks that no one could read.

All that was left on were the lights lining the path. The table had disappeared from behind the chairs.

The night that had descended was calm, cooling. Soothing, Clare felt. She wrapped herself in the shawl from her seatback. It was soothing to see the stars in the blue-black sky after witnessing such a crescendo, such an arc of noise and light. It was soothing: it was cooling.

The adults stood in a daze.

Should we expect a curtain call? Françoise was wondering.

Should we applaud? William thought. Ah, but we are too few to applaud: it would be awkward.

Yet they did applaud, led by Doug, whose sense of decorum would not have permitted otherwise. As they applauded, and then applauded some more, the groan of the garage door began, and the door descended, the dais of the coffin somehow being pulled into the garage as the door fell to. The words "fiat lux," in a Gothic script, were written on the door, the show's final message. There was to be no curtain call after all.

The adults looked around themselves anew. Lights came up in the cabin—at least one of the children had returned there.

What did you make of it? William asked to no one in particular: or, rather, he asked it to all of them at once.

I'm not sure just yet, Mike replied. It was a lot to take in.

But brilliant, just brilliant, Doug added.

Such set work, Françoise said. I had no idea that they were building such a display.

Or even that they could do so! William laughed.

It had only been an hour, and yet they could all feel that they had been transformed somehow by the experience.

Yes, yes, Clare tsked. But what did it all mean?

Corridor

August changed to September: buildings fell from the sky, were brought low. A gap filled New York like a memory of two severed fingers. Any story from this time cannot but be touched by this event. Warfare: Afghanistan and then Iraq. At home: on streets everywhere hatred seethed, guided itself in one direction or another. History will not remember us well, Michael thought, having arrived in Nottingham to begin his master's degree—the airports had all, for a few days, been closed, but reopened in time. John was sent over: to Kandahar, as an officer might expect in such times. William and Clare held their breath. Yet time ticked on: the children—adults, now—began or completed their studies. Daphne finished her degree at McGill. Celeste began hers four years later at Toronto, just when Michael came to the same university to begin his doctorate. He spent the time around his studies agitating against the war: hoping that his brother might come home. Benjamin began to step up in the ranks of the corporate world, taking some studies along the way. Helen moved to Montréal, where she lived and studied for two years alongside Daphne, in what were perhaps the happiest of their days. One night, a speeding car struck Helen down as she walked home, very late at night, or, rather, early in the morning, on Rue St-Denis. The funeral marked the first civilities between Mike and Jéanne in some years. They resumed, though with much caution, a new form of friendship. Only John, still abroad, was unable to attend the funeral. William wept openly: Clare, waking in the night, reached out for her youngest daughter, remembering all of the nights in which she checked to see if her baby and then little girl continued to breathe in the darkness. One year later, Clare's brother John, with cancer and a bad prognosis in hand, chose to end life on his own terms. Doug, now retired, sought solace in photography and travel. He departed for some time, sending only occasional missives to William and Mike, letting his brothers know that all was as well as could be hoped in Tangiers or Milan. The seasons clicked over into years. Then, once again, summer arrived.

3.

William tried to remember a line, any line, from a Canadian poem. He jumbled through the words of Robert Service—what did it mean to moil for gold, anyhow? Ah, but he'd lost the thread of the verse anyhow, the words between the rhymes.

He set Service aside and tried a different tack. E. Pauline Johnson? Something about paddles, songs.

Try again. He sometimes read the newer poetry, but seldom found much comfort in it. The contemporaries were not for him. He himself was but an anthology of aging texts, that was all. If it be not now, yet it will be. Or was it yet it will come? At any rate, Canadian lines seldom pleased him—usually seemed forgettable—the new ones as blank in verse as they were to him in meaning. Perhaps he was approaching it wrong.

And yet, here he was, as ever. Time but so thinly, its wee slices and moments shivering away from misspellings and catastrophes.

Overall, he had to admit, he was content. Things did not go exactly as planned, no, never that, but it did one no good to complain about it. He had managed to retire, after all, before the quotidian errors of his life had overwhelmed him. All of the contradictions of existing in the day-to-day felt more resolved. Perhaps that was the best that could be hoped. He had survived, somewhat against the odds, within the middle rungs of upper management at the end, and, when there seemed a clear chance to do so, he left. His pension was solid: his investments would not only outlast him: they would be a boon for his children in the time to come, with sizeable amounts to spare.

This fact was particularly true because there would be only two of them to survive him.

Failing further calamity or financial collapse.

He shuddered, resumed his walk in the undergrowth, changed his thoughts as best he could. Yet so it was: there are shadows on our souls, points that we cannot remedy, pasts that we cannot undo. So be it—let it go.

William had done as well as might be hoped, and then some. In the city it meant contributing to communities, funds for the arts or for medicine. He was due some victory laps and some slight celebration. There was even talk of a Clare Briscoe and William MacDougall wing in one of the hospitals—a modest wing, more of a corridor really—if their efforts should prove fruitful.

It was pretty good: it was enough.

William felt himself to be far from such reckoning out here at the cabin. He put on his plaid shirt, an old pair of jeans that he had left here, and his old boots. With a worn Tilley hat on his head and a walking stick in his hand, he set off on his rounds.

For all of the disappointments, for all of the heartache of things that had gone in unexpected directions, then, he was not displeased. He was, and perhaps this was the word for it, relieved. There was still so much to do, but there would always be.

He wondered—kicking over a log to find a long-disused toy car, hoary with moss and rot—if he would ever have grandchildren. It would be quite a thing. A squirrel chittered in a nearby tree. It dove down the trunk and ran off, chasing another squirrel, one that William had not spotted at first.

Yet he didn't expect grandchildren: far from it. He didn't know if he wanted grandchildren, but it would be quite a thing. Whether or not one wanted them was a question that people his age seemed to be asking themselves, as if it were their choice. Those who had grandchildren seemed pleased about it.

It was uncertain how long John would remain overseas, but William hoped that it wouldn't be too much longer. He hoped—for hoping was all that he could do—that all would be well. There was no sense fussing over it: all would come to pass. Michael was up at the cabin, and William was pleased with his son's studies, the ambitious stack of books that he had brought along with him, through which he seemed to be making good, steady progress.

William trod onward, into a part of the wood that was damp underfoot in spite of the August heat. Michael was studying something about the Holy Roman Empire, which, he had said over last night's dinner, was neither Holy nor Roman nor an Empire. It was an old joke. The details seemed to be fuzzy for his plans at the moment, except that he would be travelling to some German archives in the fall.

How William wished that he could show his sons how much time lay ahead—he remembered being their ages: the speed, the rashness that young vigour imparted. There is so much time to come—it will surprise them, William realized. The bigness of it. The space to reckon with it all. As well as its retrospective compression. Yet there could be no way to help them to see—to speed them along to recognition. Trying to warn them to prepare themselves for the long haul would be to speed them up even more, he saw.

He hoped for the best: he feared for the worst. Stepping over another bough, William saw a tiny frog hop away from him, from the shadow and into the light, before hopping again down the path and off into the grasses.

*

Michael, who was reading on the deck, could not know how his father wished for him to succeed, and how his father wished for him to do so at an even pace. He would have resented it. Yet the speed was killing him, Michael thought, pencil in his fingers, another book from his pile in his hand. He was theorizing his way out of history and toward a new way of looking at this one, more-or-less well-documented, slice of the past.

He was mired in trying to articulate the methodology of his dissertation, something that he knew he would have to figure out very soon if he wanted a chance at securing a fellowship for the next year. Every funding body seemed to love the word methodology. Why? Yet this hypothetical funding might lead to the chance to get his fledgling publications out the door. It could allow him to present at enough conferences to become recognized for what, of course, he was—all while teaching and marking those first-year student papers. The road ahead was both long and urgent.

He sat back, looked up at the aspens, up at the sky, without seeing. He took a deep breath. From the trees, he heard a woodpecker knocking against a tree. The sun was warming: it was a nice day. Would he perhaps go for a swim later?

He set himself a reading goal, told himself that he could swim after he had reached it. He didn't know how his uncle Doug had managed his long career, seeming to get out with both his hide and soul more or less intact—nor how his aunt Françoise managed hers with panache and a smile.

*

Clare looked out the window at Michael with some concern. He had grown serious—more so!—since his sister's death. He spoke well of his feelings and loss. He had delivered a tear-filled eulogy that had been the most difficult and beautiful part of the service. Yet still this loss seemed to drag him in evermore serious directions.

Oh! how Helen pulled at her heart.

Clare still disbelieved the pain that she felt, its sheer, overwhelming nature that would take over her whole being at moments. How could she ever live again? How to move, in this hurt, drawing her breath in pain, to tell the tale?

But William had retired, and they were together now. So even with John away, with Michael so far into his books, all was, after all, well— well enough. Helen's absence was palpable: Clare questioned herself daily, missed her daughter minute by minute. The feelings were physical. At times her throat was pressed beneath a weight. What could she have done? The answer, of course, was nothing.

Yet she replayed Helen's life by degrees: from birth and nursing—the long, unending nights of searing pain in Clare's breasts—through to her young, creative days. Helen seemed to have held all of Clare's happiness, her joy, her frivolity, alongside her frowning sons.

Yet she had loved them both, did not blame them, at least not on purpose. They were each quite fantastic in their own serious ways.

We do the best that we can, she sighed, wiping down the sill of the window in the kitchen through which she watched Michael read.

What joy, what pleasure awaited her? she wondered.

Of course only what joy and pleasure she could bring into her own world. She looked forward to fall in the city, to the distractions of entertaining, of being, with William, comfortably retired into gentle lives of patronage and privilege, of living well, of doing what they could to give back to a society that had granted them so much.

It was privilege, she knew: her generation had been granted comforts that might never accrue to any generation ever again. It had taken so much labour! Yet still, they had all exceeded their own expectations, and by far. It was a test now: to see how she might use it as a force for good in the world.

The smaller pleasures, then, she reasoned. Perhaps these were enough. Time would tell.

Clare turned back from the window, looking through to the dining room, where Mike and Doug were arguing about something. They were playing a game of cribbage at the table. They could argue over anything, Clare thought: just give them a topic. Clare didn't want any part of it. She was intent on reading her novel in some quiet space. Yet she was curious, as ever, as to what they were going on about. She headed in their direction as though planning to walk through the room.

The debate was about narrative.

Fifteen-two, fifteen-four—I didn't like the book, Mike said. Too flashy, too showy. It was too quick to demonstrate how clever it was. A pair makes six. It's very hard for a book to show itself for what it is—and for it still to work. But then I've never liked Ondaatje's books.

Mike had taken to reading more—he was a good reader. His pre-law degree had been in English, all those years ago. He enjoyed coming back to reading novels, writs and torts being only so interesting.

I suppose it works for me, Doug said. A run for three, a run for six, pair makes eight, fifteen-ten, fifteen-twelve. He moved his pegs along the board. There's nothing naïve to it, just a clear awareness of what's going on. Just a pair in the crib.

But I suppose that that's what strikes me as naïve, Mike cut in. A narrative that doesn't have the faith—the good faith—to stand on its own, that has to show you the tricks: it seems too uncertain, too anxious. Jejeune, even—like a child who isn't happy to show you what he's done—the tower of bricks he's built, say—but has to show you each of the steps he took to get there. Mike shuffled, dealt. If it didn't impress me on its own, showing me the steps isn't going to help much. Naïve is exactly it.

But isn't that what fiction is—the great showman, the artifice of an act we either believe in—or don't? It seems like what we get from so many books in the last twenty or thirty years is that sense that we don't have to suspend our disbelief in order to believe—we don't have to choose. Hmn. Nothing much here—there you go, Doug said, dropping two cards into Mike's crib. We all know that it's fiction, and we don't have to pretend otherwise.

He cut the deck. Mike turned up the six of diamonds. Doug led with the six of clubs.

It strikes me as sloppy, Mike said. We can do better than that.

*

Clare continued through the room, patting Mike on the shoulder as she passed. There was no need to put a word into the conversation. She headed toward the living room, where she found that her spot on the couch was both vacant and sunlit. She opened the window so that the rustle of leaves and the voices of her nieces and nephew down at the lake could drift in.

What a diminished party they were this summer! She and William and Michael—she listed in her head—Mike, Doug, and then Celeste, Daphne, and Benjamin—as well as Benjamin's fiancée, Rebecca.

Rebecca seemed sweet enough. She was someone whom Benjamin had met through a friend of a friend or something—Clare couldn't quite remember—though it was a challenge to have someone new at the cabin. And, well, really, to think of Benjamin as being so old. He was, after all, twenty-four now—the age at which, she realized, doing the math, she had divorced Daniel, just before she had met William.

Had it been a different world then? She wanted to say both yes and no at once. Her brother John—dear, lost John—had already lived for six years on his own in New York by the time he was twenty-four. Many of them had done similar things. Françoise—would that she had come this summer!—had lived in San Francisco and had already finished a degree, left for France.

She was quite sure, going back over family histories. They had all had lovers, all had had disappointment, had had lives, had been places, by that age. She would have to get used to the idea of the children having their own adult experiences, she supposed.

Oh, but they were a shrunken set, weren't they?

There was a generational shift afoot, or something like it. A chickadee called from outside the window, somewhere nearby. Benjamin's engagement was just one signal of this change. John, now that he was serving, was not about to be settled in life, and Michael, well, one would see what his PhD years brought for him. He seemed to be so tense, fraught—it did not seem like it was easy going—perhaps it was all the pressure to succeed.

Where did that pressure come from?

Clare would really just prefer that her son were happy, whatever that might mean. She was confident that his future would work out. He would be needed: he would be called to do what he would do. After all, her generation was set to retire now—wouldn't his generation be called upon to take over?

But surely at some point he might bring along a girlfriend! He hadn't done so except for once, to a Thanksgiving weekend, and that young woman, Caroline, Clare remembered her name was, had seemed quite out of sorts. Out of her element. Out of place. Michael hadn't repeated the adventure yet. He was, after all, very private by nature.

Then again, Clare thought, they were all quieter in these times.

She picked up the novel, which was where she had left it on the coffee table. The window was open: she had opened it a moment ago, she remembered. The novel was good enough: she was reading Proust, at last. But it required a lot of determination—it was hard going, and slow. She was, she thought, doing it to impress—well, herself first of all—but also Jéanne and Françoise both.

They were all still close, in spite of the years and the changes. A small part of Clare had, after all, always felt just a little bit uncultured, a little bit less intellectual, than those two women, even though part of her recognized that her reaction came from the fact that they were bilingual Montréalers by birth, and hence more worldly, while she was just another white Canadian with roots among the British Isles.

The chickadee chirruped again.

But Proust wouldn't change any of that, of course—no, she said, she was reading the book for herself. She almost believed it.

Jadis. Les jardins—maman.

It was slow. But it was time for her, too, to figure out to what had happened to all of her lost time. Part of her wished that she had gone to the bedroom to fetch her other novel, a Sophie Kinsella book, or else that book on the history of Paris that she was enjoying.

Yet Proust seemed to be the proud choice, the prudent choice. The Proustian choice. Proust was the right choice for this pensive stretch of the afternoon, the dust motes playing in the warm air, the sunbeams.

She looked out the window again at Michael, who looked up—and looked back.

How like me he is! Clare thought. They both turned to their books.

*

Doug, still over cards with his brother, did admire Proust, and he admired Clare's determination. He, too, should read Proust, he decided again, for *À la recherche du temps perdu* is what one does once retired, isn't it? Yet he hadn't really been reading all that much. Why was that?

Retirement was such an odd thing. The university had made him an emeritus, even if some of his colleagues hadn't wished it. He was used to living with quiet determination in all things. Yet retirement sat ill on him: he hung loose in its folds, like a child wearing his grandfather's tweed suit. He had at first loved it. Yet now he was losing his pace, his steady hand—he could feel it.

He dealt.

It did not do to have such doubts. He had given a great deal for his career: a determined bachelor, in the old parlance, his lovers were all men who had come through his life without overmuch affecting its contours. He had never sought all that much more. He had a wonderful, older home in Edmonton, beautifully made up and with a fantastic library. He had dinners regularly. He had many friends.

He placed an eight and a six into his own crib. Mike added two cards.

Yet he was at loose ends, in spite of being, as they say, involved in the community. He should commit to reading Proust. Perhaps doing so might help him to complete his manuscript, the first of his retirement.

If you didn't read all that much, after all, then why should you expect to be read? And how could you expect to write?

They played the hand, Mike pegging ahead of him, crossing over the skunk line.

Yet, if he added them up now, there were already a dozen books, counting those that he had edited rather than authored. It was evidence of a life lived well, he knew: he had made a contribution.

He had fourteen points in his hand—Mike had only eight.

It was a bit embarrassing for him to admit that he had never more than perused Proust.

Doug drew back into the lead with five more points in his crib, as Mike had given him a seven and a king. The cut hadn't helped.

Even if his own books hadn't exactly been bestsellers, he had made a mark: he had lived well. Yet what was he to do now? Keep on? Read Proust?

Mike dealt. Doug's hand was middling to good, depending on the cut.

It seemed, after all, that the purpose was to learn how to die well. If one had lived well, then that is what it amounted to: a good death. Perhaps he could share a bit of what he had learned along the way before his departure. He missed his students, he realized, those students who never knew just how much the professors cared about them and their futures—how much the faculty became invested in their lives. He should commit to reading Proust. He would do it.

They played the hand out. Mike won the hand—and the game—when he turned up a dozen points in his crib. Seven, seven, eight, nine. A queen in the cut.

It was time to open wine. It was time to prepare supper. The brothers got up, set to work—Clare would join them soon enough.

*

Down in the water, Daphne determined that it was up to her to make sure that someone, at least, was having fun. Benjamin, Rebecca, and Celeste were down at the lake, too.

The sun was stretching out—the leaves were rustling—it was late August, after all. In the distance they could hear motorboats in the main branch of the lake. The area was warm—nearly hot—but not quite. There was an undercurrent of chill, the hint that fall would come. It was one of those days when you could feel the change coming—one of those days where you couldn't quite be sure if it would be warmer to be in the water or out of it, on the shore or on the dock. Fish or fowl.

They had already had a canoe ride—Daphne steering in the back, Benjamin paddling up front, and Rebecca and Celeste simply riding—and they had found frogs in the rushes. The frogs were detected first by their croaking. The croaks ceased as they came closer. But then, when they let the canoe lie still, one jumped, and then another. Benjamin had spotted one swimming in amongst the grasses and then under the canoe. Celeste had seen it as well.

Daphne did enjoy the canoe, but only for short excursions. They hadn't gone far. Even though her brother was getting toward his mid-twenties, he was poor at steering. So he paddled up front, where he was still a liability, but less so. He did still wish to demonstrate some sort of manliness—or at least competence—in front of Rebecca, Daphne felt, however unconscious or unaware his impulse might have been. And Celeste, at twenty-one, was not much interested in engaging them: she was thinking, planning her next year at Trinity College in Toronto. Rebecca was not much versed in canoes and was happy to join them, observing the lake.

How interesting it was, Daphne thought, to observe someone seeing their family cabin for the first time.

Now Celeste, Rebecca, and Benjamin were on shore. Daphne watched Benjamin get up and move into the sunlight—for the sun had moved, throwing a shadow from a tall spruce across the space in which he had been sitting.

In the shade, the bugs hummed. They were talking. Their books— for they all had books with them—were held slack in their hands. Daphne's book lay on a towel. She was reading Colette—she wondered if Colette could help her to decide any of her life's next steps, now that she was a year out of university.

Well. She would swim to the dock, away from shore—swim in the late August lake, leave the muddy strand—swim a gentle breaststroke in the calm water—stand on the dock—then dive in and swim back— like they had all done when they were children. She would do as they had done when they were unafraid to enjoy themselves.

She walked into the lake, propelled herself to the dock, and stood upon it. Then Daphne dove in, away from the shoreline and its small beach. She opened her eyes—she could see well enough underwater—and looked through its hazy depths, the plant matter obscuring the distances, the light streaming down that touched the fish, the muddy sands below. She began her strokes, her head bobbing out of the water. Her brother and sister watched.

Daphne wished above all things to develop a style of her own—a certain weight of being in the world—a way of treading without causing harm. Of course she was already developing her own way through life, whether she realized it or not, she knew. But she only knew it intellectually, not emotionally, not yet.

Something flickered below her, a minnow's twirl caught in a shaft of descending sunlight. Her breathing was regular, rhythmic—even as she reached deeper water, and the lake became colder. She kept on—she swam.

Ashore, Benjamin, Rebecca, and Celeste all watched.

How I miss Helen! Celeste said.

Benjamin was not surprised: he missed her, too. For Helen had been closest to them both in age: a year younger than Benjamin, but two years older than Celeste. They had been close: they had loved their cousin.

Yes, said Benjamin. I still expect her to turn up at any moment.

I miss her smell, Celeste said. I never thought about it until she was gone.

I wish I had known her, Rebecca offered. For she had met Benjamin not long after Helen died.

Helen's was the first death—the first unexpected human death—that they had all encountered. Hers was the first death that, to them, was meaningful and significant. It was a death that let them know, at a visceral level, that they were mortal. They hurt: they mourned.

They fell to silence, hearing only the rustle of animals in the bushes and trees, the soft splash of birds on the water. Rebecca did not know what more to say. Daphne pulled herself back out of the water on the dock and waved to them. Benjamin mustered a smile: Daphne's mood no longer matched their own.

The pall that had fallen over them was temporary, however. Its mists dissipated and it was still a warm, sunny, beautiful day in which life was happy.

Daphne took a short run at the lake and then cannonballed back into the water: just like we all used to do together, Benjamin thought.

He had once imagined a world run by robots. Now he was mired in one, tied to the algorithms of computers that he did not always understand. It was not the world that he had expected it to be: most days, if he was honest with himself, he hated it. It was taking some getting used to, this adulthood thing. The condo above the river valley seemed like a paltry reward for putting up with it all. It wasn't much larger than a breadbox. Commuting was terrible, even after having moved offices. He breathed.

Daphne was already halfway back.

*

As she swam, Daphne thought of Rebecca. She had met Rebecca a couple of times before. Rebecca seemed energetic, but young. She had long, wavy, dark hair that shone red in the sun.

Something about her reminded Daphne of a downy woodpecker—the bird's precision, its flashes of red. Rebecca was beautiful in a conventional way. She had her bachelor's and master's degrees from the University of Calgary.

What else could Daphne remember as she swam? That Rebecca had studied business, marketing—something that Daphne hadn't known that you could do graduate studies in because it hardly seemed to her to be a discipline, or at least not as such—and that she worked for a non-profit agency. From what Daphne could gather, it sounded as though Rebecca spent much of her time writing the grant applications that paid her own salary. It was a situation that struck Daphne as being rather circular.

Daphne was nearing shore and would soon be able to stand.

On the balance, she liked Rebecca. She and her brother had been engaged for almost a year—it had been, she thought, a quick engagement. Rebecca was, as best Daphne could tell, just another young person doing her best to figure out and enjoy living in a difficult time on a difficult planet.

Now it was shallow once more. Daphne stood up. Her hair—it was longer these days—flopped back from her face and landed on her shoulders. The weather was so very good—it felt warm both in the water and out of it. She stepped up onto the shore and picked up her towel.

Good swim? Rebecca asked. It's such perfect weather for it.

Yes, very, said Daphne. But I feel like the old dock is such a short swim these days. Is it closer? Did Uncle William move it?

For Daphne understood these things well enough now. It was the sort of thing that William might have done with the change of the seasons, with the freeze-and-thaw of their corner of the lake, a move to keep the gulls away. She looked out and saw that there were two gulls on it—clean white gulls with yellow-orange beaks—staring back at them all on shore.

Oh no, Benjamin said with a smirk on his unshaven face, the stubble that, Daphne thought, young women are supposed to like now. It's just that we've gotten bigger. It might be further away, even. Do you remember when I was, I don't know, maybe eight, the first time I swam there? I remember feeling so triumphant, standing on it, my arms raised—and then I found that you'd beaten me to it? He turned to indicate his younger sister.

Celeste nodded, then began her own story, her memories of when the dock had seemed like it was further away.

Oh no! thought Daphne—that was not what she had meant—not at all! For a sequence of childhood stories would exclude Rebecca—who of course could not remember these things, not having witnessed them. She hadn't meant to prompt a series of nostalgic recollections.

Yet Daphne's siblings were going deeper into childhood tussles. Rebecca, quiet and beautiful, sat there smiling, seeming to listen.

*

Ah, but here was Michael. Michael would save them, Daphne thought.

Indeed, here he was, walking down the path that led from the cabin, through the spruce and aspen, and down to the dock. He had tired himself of his books, at least for now. The afternoon was getting on. And he had finished working through a dry, though interesting enough, title about the history of Carolingian writing systems. It would only touch his dissertation as a minor tangent, little more than a footnote, but his supervisor had recommended it. He deserved, he thought, a break, and so he took one, his reading quota fulfilled.

Michael walked to the dock wearing only swimming shorts, sandals, and a towel.

He has grown pale, Celeste thought, looking at Michael's hairy midriff. He almost certainly needs to get out more.

So he was doing now: he placed his towel on a bare spot on the sand, a spot nearest Benjamin. Then he lay down in the sun.

At first, everyone was silent. After a minute or so, Michael adjusted, sliding down his towel and slipping its edge up and over his eyes.

Damn, he said. Should've brought a hat.

They all sat there—or lay there, Daphne added to herself—in quiet for a while.

A small V of geese—perhaps eight or so birds—flew north overhead.

Wrong way! Celeste called after them, a cheerful singsong ringing in her voice.

The silence fell again. A few motors could be heard across the lake. Celeste worried for a moment that what she had said had been uncool. She moved on.

It was Michael who broke the silence after some time. Michael was beginning to take note of the fact that they were all, undeniably, starting to age, and he was starting to take the lead at times.

How is Aunt Jéanne? he asked. I miss seeing her here.

It was a frank, if surprising admission: as they were all in their twenties now, their habit was one of cool detachment and ironic understatement when it came to their elders. Such a clear and earnest observation was out of the ordinary.

And Françoise, too, Michael added.

Mom seems well, Daphne answered. As far as I can tell, she travels and volunteers her time to different causes. I guess the divorce settled her with enough to do that.

I like visiting her place, Celeste offered. A condo just up from Strathcona. We sometimes have girls' nights there when I am in town.

There was a pause. Michael wondered whether Celeste's siblings were invited to these nights. For instance, did Celeste's we include Daphne? Or did the visits happen in sequence? It was, though, a more or less inconsequential quibble with Celeste's sentence.

And we see Aunty Fran sometimes, Benjamin added, even though she lives over in Saskatoon. And spends a lot of her time in France. She's cool.

The conversation was an unprecedented one for them: it felt like an admission of something, though they couldn't yet be sure of what.

I like Françoise, too, Rebecca said.

Do your parents, you know, date? Michael wondered. He had never seen any evidence of his uncle Mike dating since the divorce, and he seldom saw Jéanne.

I think Mom does, Daphne said. But no one she's introduced to us, if that's what you mean.

I try not to think about it, Benjamin half-snickered, uncomfortable with the direction of the conversation.

I expect Dad does, too, Celeste added. Really, it's their business, and I'll respect that—just as I'd ask for the same.

Celeste hoped to become a teacher, she had confided in them all. Her older sister wondered if that goal wasn't making her a bit prim— as if she held some idea of what a teacher was in her head that was beginning to shape her actions. She wondered if it was as though becoming the image of a teacher could make her future unfold as she wished.

Our parents aren't as young as they used to be, anyhow, Michael said. I've started to notice them all slowing down a bit. For the most part they're as energetic as ever, he was quick to add, not wanting to alarm. I suppose I'm starting to feel like it's actually going to happen—it's actually going to fall on us, all of this grownup thing. Sooner or later, we're going to have to start taking on things around here, and back home, too.

Michael let the words sink in. He was really just trying them on, for himself, too. With his brother away, he was the eldest of them all by a year. Being responsible was perhaps starting to suit him, even if his daily life as a graduate student didn't yet give much evidence of it.

His social group on campus was crowded by young men, angry that their genius had not yet been recognized. They railed against the faculty members, perceiving them as old, foolish, and wanting. Though Michael held his doubts about these young men, alongside them he revelled. He drank too much and got high on weekends. He was dating several women, also graduate students. Even though he was open and honest with them all, even though they were all theorizing themselves into a new world to come, still, something itched near his heart.

Michael imagined that his brother and cousins likely all did some of the same. He didn't ask. He didn't need to know. His everyday was consumed with organizing political events on campus—events that he had long viewed as important—as important or more important than his life with his family.

He could see, however, and feel in himself, that change was afoot. Toronto felt very distant from the cabin, from Alberta.

I will say, he added as the pause continued, that I'm trying to help Mom now a lot more than I used to, when I'm around at least.

There was a chorus of agreement. The conversation rolled on about how their parents were aging, little signs, little pieces of evidence in the everyday.

They were pondering their collective futures, beginning in the knowledge that all of their lives were uncertain. Their time ahead was theirs to script, to begin to shape and create with conscious deliberation. They were like springtime magpies, on the wing, looking for a place to land. Their tail feathers were just growing in. For no one else would sort out their lives for them—besides the prevailing social forces. Their elders would not be there to shape the outcomes forever. Their roles were just beginning to unfasten, to unroll into another set of possible times to come.

A crow cawed from the forest's canopy. It was answered by the thrum of engines on the water.

*

Indeed, their parents were aging, but not as the children could quite yet imagine.

Mike and Jéanne both had lovers anew, as they once had had in the past. There was something very refreshing, consoling, Mike found—now out on the deck, smoking, the games of cribbage having wrapped up—about being the lover of older women. His recent partners had all been his age or older. At they aged, they wanted companionship, tenderness, and practicality. They were comfortable in their skins. They were all past—as he was—being anxious about losing their youthful good looks. They were old, and that was a welcome thing. They leaned toward the light, recognized their faults, and nevertheless strove for whatever goodness was out there.

Mike was less pursued by his demons. He had not quite overcome the folly of his desires, but life had become more about enjoying what he had, as was true of the lovers he had had in the past few years. Moreover, there seemed to be a shared reduction in their anxieties about attachment: there was less desire for things like marriage or children or even cohabitation. At his age, people had already experienced these things—or else had long since eschewed them. They didn't seem to be as compelled to bring in new complexity. He enjoyed that ease.

He was, after all, in his sixties now, and on track to retire in a few years' time, if all went according to his plans. He knew that Jéanne, too, had been enjoying aging, for he was in more contact with his ex-wife now than he had been in several years, support payments notwithstanding.

A funny thing, life was.

Mike did wish that he would have lightened and brightened up years ago, just let things slide along a bit more. But, then again, his practice had succeeded; he had done well for the children. His striving had been part of a larger aim. The children would be, already were, much freer from financial need than he had been, and that would mean that they could be freer, in turn, to choose their futures.

He stubbed out his cigarette. He did so with a twinge of regret that he had never managed either to quit or to commit to cigars. Perhaps a pipe would be the way to go as an old man. He chuckled at the thought.

A squirrel chittered in the trees, in the foliage somewhere beyond his sight, confirming the sentiment.

*

Clare, now from the kitchen, watched Mike flick his cigarette butt over the edge of the deck.

Why wouldn't he use the ashcan? Hopefully the cigarette had been properly extinguished!

But, for all that, she didn't resent him, not really. She knew that the cigarette would be out. He was conscientious. She was glad that the three brothers were so loyal to each other, were here without fail to hold each other up, bear each other along.

Yet, still, as a diminished set, a shrinking set, things were changing! Clare accepted the change, she told herself, but it felt new and awkward, like a window left open overnight.

Mike was sleeping downstairs now, in what had been one of the children's rooms. Clare had moved Benjamin and Rebecca into what had once been Mike and Jéanne's room. It was more private, after all, and the engaged young couple deserved the space. Doug, too, had moved downstairs this summer, while Daphne and Celeste were sharing his former room, which had an oversized bed. Doug and Mike were sharing the girls' old room, a room with two beds—as well as the foldout. Doug said that he preferred the cool darkness of the basement.

Well, we come home to our families, after all! Clare reasoned.

Not that any of the rooms had ever belonged to anyone, at least not in a formal way—aside from Clare and William's room, anyhow. There had just been a series of customs established over time, regular patterns into which they had settled, or perhaps, rather, fallen, like putting on a warm but frayed sweater.

To see the patterns changing was of course an inevitability, sooner or later—for they would all die one day!—but Clare had not reconciled herself to all of it just yet.

In particular, she was not quite reconciled to the muffled noises coming from Benjamin and Rebecca's room in the nighttime.

She would wash those sheets without looking too close, she thought, after they left.

And downstairs had changed, too, Clare knew well.

Once, there had been the girls' room, the boys' room, and the Other Room—the room for spillover, which was also the room with the television in it. All of that aside from the basement living room, which was a coldish room with sliding doors—the ones that worked—that let out under the deck, opening onto the path down to the water.

Now, the room that had been shared by Celeste, Daphne, and Helen—dear Helen!—was the one that Mike and Doug were sharing.

That room was large, the single bed and queen bed stretched out from one another on opposing walls. One of them could have stayed in the Other Room—for so they called it, the room with the television—but doing so would interfere with people's late-night movie watching.

Mike and Doug had shared a room as children; it was not much of an imposition for them to share one now. Clare supposed that the aging brothers enjoyed arguing themselves and each other to sleep. The only person, besides herself and William, who hadn't—who had never—changed rooms was Michael.

Michael held on in the boys' room, and just as he should, Clare thought.

It was a large room, too. It had a bunk bed and another bed, a double, across the room. Formerly, John, Benjamin, and Michael had stayed there. They did so throughout their youth. Michael had added a small table to the room, a table on which he kept his writing materials. His books were spread across the floor and on the double bed. He slept on the bottom bunk, where he always had. He said that he was glad for the room's size.

He was getting to be a bit solitary, Clare worried. He seemed to be spending most of his time alone. But not tonight! she thought.

Tonight the dinner would bring them together: tonight they would eat well, they would play cards, they would drink a few bottles of wine. Perhaps the boys—for in these moments she thought of them as boys—would dusk off the Risk board or the Monopoly set in the living room and stretch into an evening of collective play.

*

For the food was coming along: the salmon—two of them, in fact, good-sized, and brought by Doug, who had gotten them from a friend who fished off the Pacific coast—were ready to go on the barbeque on the deck. William would do the honours. The potatoes were set for roasting in trays, and all the salad wanted was dressing. Mike had even made bread, two large, plump loaves that had just come out of the oven before he had gone to smoke.

Clare was impressed by that: in spite of all of his professional demands—in spite of everything else that he had been doing so far today, too—he kept up in the kitchen. He cared a great deal whether the yeast rose or fell. He leaned into his dough, into the task of kneading. She had heard him advising his son, too, on the bread, just as Benjamin and Rebecca had been heading out the door, down toward the water.

Clare admired Mike, after all, and Doug, too: they contributed. Everyone did. No one was perfect, but they did what they could.

Clare sighed. In the end, she thought, we ought to make ourselves smaller, quieter—we must be gracious as we let the younger generation take over. We need no longer to be needed. Soon, we will need them instead.

She picked up her wine and headed toward Proust and the living room just as William passed through on the landing.

Well, off to the dump, he said. Anywhere I've missed?

I'm not sure, Clare answered. Did you remember the bathrooms?

Oh yes, of course.

And the garage? Weren't there a couple of bags in there?

Oh yes, right. Of course. William went down the stairs.

How much inflection tells us! Clare thought. William's two sentences had been nearly the same, yet opposite in meaning.

A couple of minutes later, Clare heard the engine of the truck turn over, fail, turn over again, fail again and fail better, and then start. Third time is the charm, she thought. Lucky that that truck is still running at all.

*

Downstairs and outside, William felt much the same. As the engine turned but did not start, he felt a moment of terror—what would happen if it would not start at all? A northern flicker flew up from the brush and away from the truck as the engine shuddered, the bird's orange underparts starting to blend into the changing hues of the trees.

Was it the starter? The alternator? Or was it one of the mysteries of the engine—all of those things under the hood?

William did not know, not in any meaningful way, how engines worked. The mechanisms of machinery were where his usual command, his control, left him. But he did love the bright flight plumage of the flicker. He had had the truck serviced before in the nearby town, and more than once, but he never enjoyed the process, the man-speak that he faked.

So the engine's eventual start-up was a distinct pleasure: he felt the moment of fear pass, felt the flood of comfort return to his body. All was well. He put the truck into gear and rolled along the driveway, the gravel popping under the truck's tires.

The drive was going to be a hot one. William opened the window by the time he had reached the end of the driveway. He reached across the bench seat to crack open the passenger's side window as well. The children were down at the water. He turned right at the end of the gravel, and then, a couple of minutes later, at the stop sign, he turned right again.

We can turn left later, William thought.

He drove at a modest pace, the breeze coming in at the window. It was quiet: he listened to the leaves, to the sounds of the truck—its six cylinders revolving or firing or whatever it was that they did— generating the power to propel him and his family's refuse onward. He would have to drive to the dump once more before they left for the season, but perhaps that final load would be—it should be—small enough to leave it in a dumpster on the way back south to the city.

So this trip could be it for the truck this summer, he supposed.

He should consider selling the pickup, he realized. Not that doing so was really worth his time or effort. It would be worth next to nothing—very little. Perhaps one of the children might want it, but then, of course, they were urban dwellers—or else overseas, in John's case. None of them were going to have much use for a rusty half-ton.

He drove along, the lake at first peeking out from behind the cabins, then fading from sight as the road headed onward, toward the dump. The leaves rustled: it was hot out. Insects thrummed in the shade.

In a few minutes, William arrived. It was a quiet day at the dump. There were a couple of rough-hewn new signs that he drove past without looking as he crossed the tracks. The dump was otherwise much the same. He drove in, waved at the manager, or whatever his title was—William had never taken the time to find out—and followed the signage toward the current dumping grounds.

The older phrase, nuisance grounds, passed through his mind.

It was hot and sunny—birds were singing in the shade of the trees. Bugs were buzzing. All was well with the world.

William parked the truck and got out, feeling the sun warm up his mackinaw and then reach through to warm his tired skin. He stood for a moment, his back heating up against the skies. It was a beautiful day and, yes, all was well with the world.

He stepped up into the box of the truck. The garbage was self-contained—it was an easy job. One by one, minding his back, he lofted the bags into the heap. There were no bears today, he noticed, either inside or outside of the fence. Perhaps they were nearby. He had read that the bears had started to become aware of when hunting season began in the fall, and that they were now heading deeper into the woods by that time, toward the mountains. Hunting season was still a little ways away, though. William didn't doubt that the bears could sense the danger that the humans posed.

They could be in the trees somewhere today, waiting for nightfall.

As he heaved the last bag—for the most part food remnants—the bag tore in mid-air, spilling out a juice of decomposing fruits and vegetables, bones from a side of ribs that Doug had barbequed a few nights ago.

The detritus fell toward the ground and the bag sailed onward, landing with a half-full thwump amidst a pile of other waste. It sailed like a ship of sickened passengers in wartime, half-emptied and limp as they reached the blasted shore.

What a world, William thought. We deserve it, though: to be killed by wanton gods for their sport.

Yet it was beautiful: all was good, kind, and crisp. It was summertime. All was well—and yet mean.

Crows looked up and saw the torn vessel landing in the rubbish. Two took to the air with lazy flaps of their wings and began a closer inspection.

William climbed back out of the box. He stepped up into the truck. There was the bulldozer. William thought of derelict buildings, rubble, then waved at the dump manager, who was starting up the machine. William started the truck as well, and then headed toward the exit.

*

It was after the exit, as he approached the road again—that short stretch of gravel in the trees, perhaps two hundred metres in length, bisected by the tracks—that William felt overcome by grief.

He pulled the truck to the shoulder. A small ditch ran beside the road past the level crossing. The world sounded joyful outside. Water moved in the ditch, running toward a stream, a river, a lake.

He tried not to think of groundwater contamination, agricultural runoff.

Helen should be with him.

William burst into tears.

Loud, sobbing howls pushed up from places that he seldom let loose. He pulled back, then let the pain wash over him. His nose ran, and he let it, mopping it with the sleeve of his mac.

He felt so alone with Helen gone. Most days he couldn't bear to think of it. So he didn't. Yet here was the dump that she had adored. Perhaps the bears had always come just for her. Would there ever be bears again? Would the world be alright?

William's tears flowed as they had on the terrible day of Helen's funeral, when he broke down afterward, in the quiet evening. How could such a thing have happened to Helen? His beautiful girl, whom he remembered with such clarity and fondness from the moment of her birth? She had crawled and then walked beside him so steadfast for her twenty years, only to end in a flash of headlights, far from home.

William had tried for anger, anger at the driver who had killed her, anger at the Montréal in which she had died, anger at the friends who had been with Helen that night. He had tried for anger at himself, at Clare, for having encouraged her to go so far for her studies.

But no, he only had loss: loss and sorrow.

Three years now, almost, and yet he was overwhelmed with sadness to find himself here, at the dump, by himself. He had so loved Helen's simple delight in the place. In her absence, the happy humming of the insects and the merry stirring of the leaves were the worst insults.

Damn the crows and damn the gulls. Everything left him feeling bereft.

William mopped his eyes, his nose, with tissues from the crushed box that he found under the bench seat—a box that would have been in the truck when Helen last rode in it—and he was glad that no one else had driven by.

Why be so sad now? Clare's brother John had died since then, and by his own hand, too, after that fateful prognosis.

William felt, though, that John had already long since left them: Helen was supposed to be here still. It was all a dreadful mistake. William to this day found himself imagining Helen turning a corner and coming to greet him with the open smile that she reserved for her father. For months after her death, he saw her everywhere that he went.

Yet he must go on: it was his duty to continue, for John and Michael's sake, and for Clare's sake above all. They had grieved: they had lost their daughter. It had been a strain, yes, but the family came together to mourn, to move through the melancholy that set in in the aftermath.

Now William found himself, under a late summer canopy of birch leaves, with the birds twittering in the branches, on a gravel road by the dump, next to the railroad, once again overcome by the loss. A robin sang.

He should have passed before Helen: that would have been right. To imagine that her hands—he imagined her child-sized hands in his own, years ago—would never touch the earth again, would never make anything new, would never palm gently into his own hands again: that, to William, was agony.

Yet he must go on: he wiped his eyes again and looked about, glad that still no one had driven past. He leaned toward the open window, breathed in, out. The world continued: so would he.

There were things to do. William had survived his career: he was beginning what could be a long retirement. His next existential task was to learn how to die well. It would be neither a simple task nor a quick one. He had to render himself obsolete, make space for his children to come into their own.

He also had time left, he hoped, to make his small corner of the world a little bit better than he had found it. He might do so, too, provided that the government did not plunge them into war on many fronts, did not destroy environmental laws and civil rights—the world could be left, perhaps, just a little bit improved.

You are on Native land. William saw these words on one of the signs by the level crossing. It was a new sign.

Yet the globe was hardening: people were hardening, too. William, in his retirement, hoped to soften the edges: he no longer had to be so firm, so quiet, patient, and proper. Yet of course it had become habitual by now. Nevertheless: he had survived his career. He would have to find out what that sign signified. He could be part of making the world better—he was part of making the world better.

Would Helen recognize him now? He pushed the thought away.

He turned the truck back on, put it into gear. The drive would help him to refresh: the breeze through the windows could lift his spirits, even if Helen wasn't there any longer to accompany him in silence.

He hoped that her death had not been too painful. Yet what did he know of pain? Beyond a root canal and having once broken his arm—years ago, as a child—he knew nothing of pain. It was alien to him, something that he had seldom experienced.

He drove. The trees whispered. The birds provided the melody, while squirrels scampered in the leaves. As he got closer to the cabin, he saw, along the shoulder of the road, his two brothers walking: Doug had his camera and was quiet and calm, while Mike loped alongside him, ambling, loose, talking, gesticulating.

Perhaps he could join them, William thought. Though first he would see to Clare, see what wanted doing inside, perhaps work together on cooking the evening meal. What was it again tonight? Pasta? Steak? No, fish, William remembered: he would be cooking the salmon.

*

Mike turned from the pickup as William passed, the dust from the road landing on his back. Doug waved with one hand. He protected the camera with the other.

Doug did enjoy his camera—he enjoyed the aging technology, one that he knew would soon be obsolete. He worked with an older Canon model, shooting in 35mm film that he had learned to develop himself in a repurposed room in the basement of his Belgravia home.

Many of his colleagues wondered why he hadn't left Edmonton upon his retirement, as most people seemed to do, but he loved his home. He loved his life in Belgravia, a quiet neighbourhood named for a part of London and that was in very few respects similar to the original. He was part of the city, part of a community.

He enjoyed the patience of film: he was learning how to be patient again. He was at the moment carrying his most basic setup: the camera had a fixed 55mm lens with a polarizing filter, no more. 400 ISO colour film.

What was he shooting for? He shot for himself, for the stillness of his basement darkroom, and for the unexpected results that sprang up on the contact sheets that he printed. Perhaps the images would amount to something—perhaps they wouldn't. It didn't matter if there were results. That fact was in itself a tremendous relief after all of the years of watching the university shift until it seemed to care for little else but the results—for those cold, hard, quantifiable outcomes, learning and thinking be damned.

Doug was old enough to know that his camera work was really a hobby, nothing to be taken too seriously—that his serious work, for what it was worth, lay in the manuscript that he toiled away on in his study in the mornings, the manuscript that he trusted would be completed within the next year or so. Even that, though, was his choice.

The camera gave him a point of focus that took his mind elsewhere. It was portable, it was material, and it was technical—all things that he enjoyed and had admired in others' skills and arts before he retired.

At first, he had imagined himself doing portraits—something like Mapplethorpe, but not quite so shocking. But as an old man living in Alberta's capital—even with its sometimes-gritty edge—he knew that he wasn't the same as a young man living a flashy life in another era in New York City.

He did admire the black and white portraits and self-portraits that he had completed. The self-portraits, in particular, were his favourites. These documented the sagging skin, the awkward stubble, the slow fade of an aged white man who drank two morning espressos and who liked little more in the world than to share a bottle of wine. Like a wise and wizened old turtle, a wrinkling man in a turtleneck, he thought of himself.

By and large he was too embarrassed to ask people to sit for him, but David, a long-time friend and sometime lover, had turned out to be a fair subject for him, too—two old men connecting across the ravages of time, survivors of many difficult years.

He felt little compunction to apologize for any of it anymore—for his gay life, which everyone knew about but no one really wished to discuss, especially he himself—but neither was his life as rebellious, or as dangerous, as it once had been. Or once had seemed, at least.

He took a deep breath and looked down the road on which he and Mike were walking. His thinning hair felt gritty.

Today's setup would just allow him some broad pastoral shots and portraits, nothing specialized or too interesting. He stopped, removed the lens cap, then put the camera up to his eye.

Mike was not quite pausing: he was walking along the edge of the road, where a neighbour had laid railway ties to demarcate the edge of his property. The ties were rotting. Ants strode in their orderly manner in the sunlight that baked the wood. Mike stepped along the crumbling beams, playful, one foot on the tie, the other in the air.

Doug was glad to see that his brother was regaining his sense of joy— he seemed to be lighter than he had been in a long time. Doug turned the camera from the poplar that he had been investigating, looking for the birds that he could hear all around them, and looked at his brother. He wished that he had had more lenses with him, or a bit of zoom, either out or in. A macro lens would allow for good shots of the plant life, which was just passing its late summer peak, but that was beside the point.

The camera showed Mike in a medium shot, from about the waist up, teetering, smiling, unshaven, his bit of stubble caught in the sunlight along with his greying, brown hair.

Doug focused, snapped several shots, advancing the film each time with his thumb. Click, click, click went the shutter. The crickets chirped. Doug enjoyed the feeling of the mirrors snapping in place inside the body of the camera.

Mike fell from the last of the ties, landing on his feet back on the gravel on the shoulder of the road. He worried about crushing ants and wood bugs underfoot.

Doug lowered the camera and smiled.

They walked on. Sometimes they chatted, sometimes they were quiet—the difference didn't much signify any longer: they were brothers, and they were close. That was enough.

Doug finished his film cartridge, wound it up, and unpacked it from the body of the camera. They headed back toward the cabin. Although he would never know it, one of the images that he had captured would be used, some seventeen years later, to commemorate Mike upon the event of his death.

*

As they regained the cabin, life was picking up steam: it felt busy. Everyone was congregating upstairs. Celeste, Daphne, and Rebecca were setting the table, sipping wine, and laughing. They had miscounted, putting out ten settings when there should only be nine. This mistake had become the source of some hilarity.

Benjamin and Michael were playing cribbage, but without much conviction—the elder Mike could see that his son was aware that he, too, should have been helping. His nephew Michael seemed to feel the same.

In the kitchen, Clare was pulling things from the fridge—salads, the salmon—and bringing the accoutrements out and setting them on the table in the dining room. Another bottle of white went into the fridge.

Mike stepped outside with a glass of the wine that his daughter handed to him. It was something from the Okanagan region. The sliding glass door made an angry noise.

William was out there now, warming up the barbeque, a large, new grill that he had bought this year to replace the small, rusted one that had been at the cabin for perhaps twenty years. The sun was still high, but it was beginning to dip westward, down toward the lake.

Mike sipped. Good day for it, he said.

Yes, it certainly is, William agreed.

Might go for a paddle tomorrow. Want to join? Mike asked. Doug and me. Nothing too serious. Probably just for the morning, so a simple round the lake.

Hmn, answered William. Probably, depends, but I can't see why not. It would be nice to have a last crack at it before we pack up.

Exactly. Mike sipped again.

There was a pause now, a lull in the conversation. From the deck, the two brothers looked westward, the sun shining on the lake beyond the trees.

How you doing these days? Mike asked.

Most of the conversations at the cabin were kept light, were held in passing. But they were checking in on each other, too, when they could. Each trip, in the end, was a version of such a check-in, a demonstration of continuity that showed that everything was alright in a changing world.

Yet these earnest moments were important for them, too. William felt himself to be at a loss.

I think I'm okay, he said at length. I never expected that I would bury any of my children. Clare's brother's passing was okay, but Helen—I just don't know what to make of it. Still.

He surprised himself by being more or less articulate, but perhaps it was because he had already broken down once today. It had been the first time in months. He found that he could speak about it now.

Even though it was a long time ago, I'm surprised at how it hurts still. Though I feel like I'm finally letting it go, accepting. Or something, William added.

Having children is terrifying, isn't it? Mike said. All of the idiocy of being young needed to find a way to end when I became a dad. Mike smiled now, remembering. But we kept true enough to each other—I thought that I had some idea of what to expect. I never expected to be divorced at this age. I never expected how much I would need, or want, my children to help me. I thought it was the other way around, that I would just let them go one day. I had no idea.

Me neither, William agreed. But it's put a lot of things in perspective. I feel like I do little else than spout clichés. They grow up so fast, et cetera. Except that none of the clichés are about our children dying. I had no idea what it took to be a dad —

*

At this point the door slid open with a grind. Doug held out two cedar slabs, one in each hand, a huge salmon on each.

Mike stepped over to grab one. Doug pushed the door open, the track underneath it complaining all the while.

Ready? Doug said.

William opened the barbeque, the heat hitting his face. They arranged the fish, then closed the lid.

Doug went inside, then came right back out again, a glass in hand.

Nice day, he said, without either meaning or weight.

Yup, Mike agreed. Good time for three old farts to enjoy a patch of sunshine. He turned his face to the sun. Three years to go until I retire, he added. Then there'll be no stopping us.

Ha, Doug snorted. On our scooters. He looked a little bit tired. It takes a lot to keep going, some days, he said.

His brothers remembered the years—they remembered the things said and the things that remained unsaid.

Yes, William agreed. I try to remind myself every morning that waking up is privilege enough and that I should be happy.

Okay, that's bleak, Mike said. Have you heard from John? Things are getting pretty heavy in Afghanistan.

Stupid war, Doug said. We should never have been part of it.

At this point, the conversation dove into the politics of Iraq and Afghanistan, intermingled with the long shadow of September 11th. It seemed to be a hopeless mess.

Doug and Mike got going, and it was the hypotheticals—well, what do you think we should be doing instead? Mike prodded Doug—that William most enjoyed hearing them debate.

Even though this conflict touched their family personally, with John's being imperilled every day now, there was still a rhetorical element into which they could sink their teeth. There were always so many things about which to disagree, after all.

Think of the future, Doug said. Will our grandchildren—well, your grandchildren—one day be reading about 9/11 as the beginning of the Third World War? Or did it start with the first Iraq war? What was the Franz Ferdinand moment that started it all? I don't expect that history is going to look kindly on any of us.

William thought back to the pageant five years ago.

And to be frank, Doug added, we'll deserve it.

Mike launched back, an inquiry into whether there was such a thing as a moral universe—whether such a difficult idea as civilization still held any meaning—and, if so, if we could grant that there was such a thing as right or wrong, how we should then proceed.

*

Clare could hear the three brothers from inside the kitchen.

How well they all got on these days!

She was pleased that these simple bonds held them so. She thought of her brother—of his leaving, of his intermittent presence in her life. She still hadn't made up her mind as to whether his suicide had been selfish, or whether he had spared himself—and all of them—the suffering of his final illness.

He had left her behind! her inner voice exclaimed.

For a moment she felt like a child, abandoned in a large, clean room with all of the toys—free to play, but to play only in isolation. Yet she couldn't decide, really, if it was suicide at all, or just a hastened death. She chilled at the thought of her own eventual passing—what would that final darkness feel like as it descended?—but there was a salad to dress.

Michael, can you ask your father how long it will be? she called out.

Michael looked up. Just a moment, he said.

For Benjamin was about to lay down a hand that would win him the game. Sixteen points for a come-from-behind victory. Michael nodded, stood up. Benjamin did the same.

When will they learn to put away their own toys? Clare wondered.

But it mattered little. Everything was abuzz. She had figured out how to include the boys, who, on their way to the deck, each pulled a bottle of beer from the fridge.

Benjamin pushed the door open. It ground along in its track, proclaiming its misery.

I must ask William to see to that! Clare thought, once again to herself.

Benjamin and Michael went out and joined their fathers and uncles on the deck, where the salmon was starting to cast a fantastic scent into the early evening air.

*

Mom wants to know how long, Michael said to his father.

Oh, about eight, ten minutes yet, William answered.

Michael stepped back to the door, repeated William's words to Clare, Daphne, Rebecca, and Celeste inside, then ground the door shut.

Menfolk and womenfolk, Michael observed. Yet it seemed natural enough, and they mixed in all sorts of ways at different times. It was, wasn't it, natural enough? He couldn't decide. It felt off.

He walked back toward the others, toward the railing that looked down to the lake. Both he and Benjamin pulled from their beers.

Read anything good today? Doug asked Michael.

From almost anyone else—Benjamin in particular, or from his absent brother, perhaps above all of the rest—this question would have rankled him. But Michael respected his uncle as an academic who had come before him, who understood what it all meant.

No, not really, was Michael's answer.

Ah, but you're learning how to read in grad school, Doug said. Quickly, brutally—no real sentiment attached to it. Finish a book, move on to the next one. Much less romantic than we were taught to believe. Takes some of the fun out of it, but it gets the job done.

Yeah, suppose so, Michael said, then sipped.

There was a pause. Michael continued. It does make me wonder why we bother, each of us, to spend so much time and care, if someone is just going to come along, read fast, read just in order to critique, and then move on. Why should I take so much time in the writing—why should I care so much—if that's really the best that can be hoped for?

The insects buzzed, and the motorboats, too.

Well, wait and see, William interjected, wanting to reassure his son.

The trees kept their weight and their silences.

You might be surprised, Doug said. I've been moved by the care that some of my readers took over the years. I've felt like I didn't often have the time or the luxury to take such care myself. It was humbling to get such responses. I didn't always, or even often, feel like I deserved the attention, or that my work did, anyhow. I'm very grateful for what my readers gave me without expectation of a return.

He paused a moment.

I don't have too many illusions anymore: I'm not a flashy academic, not a particularly bright star shining above the ivory tower. Nor am I a best-selling writer. But I've put some words on the page, and some people have read them, and they got enough out of the experience that they took the time to let me know that it meant something to them. That's enough, really. But it takes time.

The conversation drew a long breath.

Patience it is, then, Michael said, raising his bottle.

Benjamin did the same. The brothers raised their wineglasses. For a moment, a comfortable silence descended on them, and they looked toward the water.

*

Inside, Clare handed the last things to Rebecca and then looked out the window at the men. There were still a couple of minutes left by her reckoning. William hadn't yet lifted the lid on the gleaming steel of the barbeque.

She turned and watched Rebecca, who was placing the basket of buns that Clare had handed to her onto the table. It wasn't the right place for the basket, but no matter. Rebecca's movements were a little bit tentative, Clare thought, as she analyzed how the three young women interacted with each other. But, then again, Rebecca was in alien territory, with the whole family watching her. Clare would be tentative, too, in the same circumstances.

Even though Benjamin had introduced Rebecca to the family a couple of years ago, the change still seemed new. Clare observed that

Daphne and Celeste seemed to like her—they seemed close enough. They spoke together—they laughed.

Clare turned back to the kitchen: were all of the condiments out? She opened the fridge to make sure.

Celeste was also observing Rebecca.

Such dark hair! So much of it! It would be wonderful hair to have, she thought.

She could still remember a time when she thought that her own hair was just about perfect. She had been younger then.

Celeste liked Rebecca well enough. She didn't know her well, though—she was too busy with her studies to have really gotten to know her brother's fiancée. Rebecca and Benjamin lived in the city now, west of what Celeste thought of as the core, in some condo in Oliver, which was a cultural light year away from her life on campus in Toronto. Plus, Rebecca was two years older, Benjamin three. Celeste loved her brother, and she loved her family, but she was happiest to see them, for the most part, at those times that were confined to holidays and the cabin.

Except for her mother, whom she missed.

Benjamin had driven down with Rebecca, separate from the rest of the family. He drove a tidy banker's Volkswagen that demonstrated that he had both enough money and taste—as well as restraint—to do well for himself. Yet she loved him, and in turn this woman who was to become her sister-in-law.

Celeste's thoughts, however, were interrupted as a sudden parade of men brought two steaming salmon into the house, like cavemen returning from the hunt.

Or was it just two huge fillets? Daphne could not quite see, but, either way, she could tell that it was a lot of fish. The dinner would be a rowdy one at this rate, she thought, as they were already somewhat into their cups.

Daphne enjoyed being able to drink around her parents and relatives now—she was old enough that it was no longer anyone else's concern. The same held true for her elders, she imagined. They were old enough now to be able to be more human—more flawed, more vulnerable— around the children. Daphne appreciated the shift, watching both her mother and father, piece by piece, setting down the defensive armour that had gotten them through the thickest years of their living and of their parenting. Her aunt and her uncle, too, even if their shift had been brought on by grief over Helen's death.

The salmon was laid on the table: Doug did the honours of cutting it, of serving it.

A new bottle of wine was uncorked—a night for a nice, light white! Clare felt—and the dishes were filled.

Plates were piled high: salads were sent around, fish, potatoes, buns. Mike went to refill the butter dish. Loaves. Butter. Dish. Salt.

From his end of the table, William looked at them all and was satisfied. Each person and each item was a portrait, still-life, or still alive. It was enough: yes, indeed, this moment: it was enough. He could die happy.

Sooner or later, every famous man would amount to no more than a forgotten and weathered tombstone at best. Each in his narrow cell forever laid. He was not famous, he was not rich—well, not overmuch—but he was, at this moment, happy. Look on my works, ye mighty, and despair! It was enough.

Doug passed him the bottle of wine: William refilled his glass. He passed the bottle along. Then he took some potatoes.

Down the table, Mike raised his glass.

For our hosts, he said. And, once more, to patience. May it see us through.

There were echoes, murmurs, and clinkings all down the table.

Yet what did that mean, patience? Clare wondered, her glass chiming off Celeste's, then Michael's. But she was soon swept into the dinner, into a meal that was, by any measure, one of the cabin's triumphs. How much food determines our fortunes!

*

As dinner wound down, the men got up to clean. Mike stepped out for a smoke. The sun was not down yet, but it would be soon.

Clare, Daphne, Celeste, and Rebecca were left at the table, with Benjamin ferrying plates to the kitchen and opening a new bottle of wine.

Benjamin was, all of a sudden, thinking of robots. He no longer believed that they would save the day. Really, he knew now, his job at the bank was more or less one of managing the robots—the machines that did all of the calculations. He had trained enough—and had trained enough people, too—to know how to do his job, and how to do it well. He interfaced with people with efficiency and tact. Then he presented their desires to the robots that controlled them all. So he managed the robots, and was paid well for it, too.

But he remembered his childhood confidence in the future—and he missed his cousin, the cousin whom he had seen here in the summertime and in the holidays. He picked the salt and pepper shakers up from the table and carried them into the kitchen. Soon he would buy a home and keep the condo as an investment, he thought, moving the pieces into place.

What would come next? That was what Celeste wanted to know.

The evening was going, tripping and traipsing along, and she was tipsy from the wine. Celeste enjoyed being tipsy. Her sister was tipsy as well, she could see. Benjamin did not seem to be tipsy.

Tip, tip, tip—see? Did Aunt Clare? Seem tipsy? She couldn't tell, but then again her aunt had so much more experience with these things, didn't she? Celeste was hoping that there would be a loud, riotous card game—and more wine.

Daphne was hoping for the same, though perhaps with less riot. She had grown to treasure—yes, treasure, she told herself—these evenings with her family. For things could change overnight. Funny, though: if any of them, she had expected that it would be John, in Afghanistan, who wouldn't make it. Things could change so fast—so unexpectedly.

Daphne supposed that that was one of the lessons of adulthood. It was not an easy lesson. Make the best plans possible and trust in the future—while knowing that it might disappear in an instant. So, yes, she hoped for a game. She sipped her wine.

*

In the kitchen, the men were making brisk business of the dishes. Doug was washing and Michael was drying. Benjamin was restocking the fridge, placing each jar or bottle back in its place.

Mike, in from his smoke—the door grated so on one's nerves! Clare thought—was putting the dishes away.

William took to the sidelines and cheered them on. Truth be told, he was tired. Not that it had been such a tiring day, but still, he was tired. He poured scotch for anyone who wanted it: Doug and Mike said yes, and Michael surprised him by asking for a tumbler as well, neat.

Benjamin opened another beer.

The conversation was oriented toward the practical—pass that dish! Look out, I'm opening the fridge door!—and so on.

William wondered if they weren't all holding something in: holding something back. For himself, he felt purged, wrung out from his trip to the dump, from his afternoon on the deck, from a hot, clear day at the cabin. He knew that he would sleep well. He didn't feel like he was holding back, because he had already let it out. He wondered, however, if there wasn't a sort of speechless quiet in the room now, something that he couldn't quite place.

After a few minutes more, William stood up, took a rag, and wiped down the table. Clare, Rebecca, Daphne, Celeste, and now Benjamin, who had sat down, all lifted their drinks in turn, then set them back down as he passed.

Their glasses would all leave rings in the damp that William had left behind. One couldn't help it, so it was best to accept the circumstances assigned by fate. Coasters were but a needless encumbrance.

And now, William saw, the children were organizing for games. He didn't think that he had it in him, not this evening. Perhaps something more sedate—a film: something more or less mindless.

Doug looked just as un-keen. William thought that perhaps they might take their scotches downstairs and watch something tasteful enough to suit his erudite brother, but light enough for his mood.

Michael, too, looked like he wasn't feeling social. William wondered whether his son would join them downstairs for a film, or whether Michael would return to his books, as so often he seemed to be doing. William hoped for at least the sociable companionship of a movie.

He began to move downstairs—he broke the circle and opened the space for each to determine their next steps.

They split as he had predicted: Michael and Doug both declined the games on offer.

This arrangement would leave Clare, Mike, Benjamin, Rebecca, Daphne, and Celeste.

The perfect number for a game of canasta! Clare said.

Benjamin had been hoping for enough people to break into two games—he had been hoping to have enough willing players for a game of Risk.

Rebecca looked unsure of herself, tipsy as she was, too, and not quite certain of all of the rules of the card game into which she was being dealt.

Yet the actions all seemed to unfold as though through long rehearsal and practice: many of the details didn't need thorough articulation. The men went to the Other Room downstairs. The six players found a new bottle of wine, drew up their chairs, found the cards, as well as a score sheet, and began dealing.

Rebecca did, in the end, need to be reminded of the finer points of the rules several times. Benjamin kept himself from being frustrated by her lack of easy grasp. At some point later on, William came upstairs and made large bowls of popcorn for everyone. The evening proceeded—all was well—the family continued—time passed—and, one by one, everyone went to bed or fell asleep.

Tomorrow and tomorrow and tomorrow, Clare muttered to William as they both arrived in bed. Outside, coyotes were braying and yipping down the lake.

To the last syllable of recorded time, William answered.

Corridor

We must smile and laugh while we can, for time is a cruel keeper. It passes as quick as ever: it accelerates the headlong rush to the grave. William, at sixty-seven, died one night of a stroke. It was sudden and it was merciful. Had he been asked, he would have wished to have come to some greater sort of peace before it happened. He would have wished to set aside his sorrows and to have laughed more with Clare. And yet. He passed just before John could return from Kandahar, a new, yet also unchanged, man. He would never tell all that he had seen there. There could be no telling. Michael's doctoral defense, however, was told at length: it was accounted to be one of the strongest that the History Department at the University of Toronto had seen in many years. Yet now, three years out of his studies, he was unemployed, again, as September loomed. It hadn't helped that he had completed his degree just as the stock market collapsed, taking with it much of the government spending that underwrote the university system. The public sector everywhere crouched, ducked, and groaned under the buzzword of austerity. And yet. Things changed: things stayed the same. One morning, Mike woke up and decided to join his brothers in retirement, choosing a swift exit from his firm. It was, he felt, the second-best decision that he had made. The best was, at last, to have apologized to Jéanne—for all of his many shortcomings. They were resuming, after many years and much wandering, a new, uncertain, yet deep and affirming time together. His third-best decision, in his own reckoning, was to have quit smoking. Françoise was pleased to see her sister happy again—it also meant that she could, with more ease, see her nieces and nephews. She could rejoin the family at the cabin, where mobile phones were all put away and, for the first time in a long time, they all—well, the twelve of them, including the baby, Max; thirteen if one included Benjamin and Rebecca's dog, Sarah—found the time to be there together. The cabin had lain in quiet rest for some time: no one had been up in months. Clare called in advance, as was her habit. The old cleaner from town had retired, but her daughter had taken over the business. She went ahead of them all, clearing the dust and cleaning up where the mice had gotten in over the winter and opening the windows to let in the air from the lakeshore. The air brushed the curtains and woke the place up, once again.

4.

All that is solid melts into air, Michael thought, the truck bumping along beneath him. But what solids do melt into air? he wondered, trying to recall any. Something must, because otherwise where did Marx get that idea?

The truck rumbled as Michael turned right at the stop sign.

Nitrogen? Or more immediate things? Did, for instance, his father melt into air? Their memories of him? Everything that he had done, every deed? Michael remembered the time after his father's passing. His mother's shock and horror to wake up one day and find her husband of almost thirty-eight years dead in the bed beside her.

While his uncle Mike had been William's executor—handy to have a lawyer in the family, Michael had then realized—Michael had taken on much of the practical work. He had defended his dissertation and was teaching only a single course in Mississauga. From afar, he helped as he could. He cancelled some classes to fly home.

The angry young men from his cohort, leaving with their master's degrees, had largely abandoned him. They went elsewhere to start their doctorates or else did not complete them in Toronto. John hadn't been able to return from Kandahar until two months later. So Michael had managed the details, tidied his father's things, and delivered another eulogy.

How many of those things from his father's life, how many solids, had melted into air? What had Michael simply gotten rid of, hadn't thought twice about, that his father had cared about deeply?

None of this philosophizing was the meaning that Marx's sentence had held in its original context. Yet Michael felt that it was somehow fitting as he drove along past the cabins.

The truck was firing well enough. John had seen to it—John had learned many useful skills along the way, Michael granted. And now he was a veteran, part of a new generation of veterans in the making.

Michael thought of Carolingians and Merovingians, of the patterns of ancient warfare that had gripped the world since its early days. Perhaps every generation needs to have its war so that there are those who can remember how dreadful it is, he thought. Or else we forget and start the cycle all over again. Perhaps, in fact, that was what we had just done.

He looked out the window, sighed into the leaves. He dearly hoped to get news, soon, about his fall teaching—he hoped for a less disastrous schedule than last term's sprint between campuses. He didn't think that he could do it again.

The truck smoothed out on the road now, the asphalt under the tires. It bobbed up and down on its springs. Michael drove along, looking through the trees. A crow cawed. He would check his phone when he arrived at the store, see if any emails had arrived to confirm his courses, even if doing so was a breach of the shared family agreement to shelve their devices for the trip.

The leaves flickered past. He patted the pocket of his shirt one more time to check that he had the grocery list prepared by his mother and aunts. It was there, folded up in the breast pocket of this old plaid flannel piece.

How odd it felt to be driving the truck! Michael found that he was quite enjoying doing so.

He passed his brother, who was out on his run. Benjamin was with him, though labouring in John's wake.

Michael stuck his hand out the window as he passed. It was acknowledgment enough. He had decided to set down his resentment of his older brother—for John had suffered. Solidarity was better than strife, even though the two maintained irreconcilable politics. The realization had come to him when their father died: it was time to grow up.

Michael fiddled with the knobs on the radio, checked to see if he might be able to find a station amidst the ups and downs of Lacombe County. He passed a few static-filled stations with contemporary music, country music. At length, he found the CBC. It came in with relative clarity.

Funny, Michael thought, that his father hadn't used the radio in the truck—otherwise it would already have been tuned to the CBC. Someone else could have changed it, but the truck had seldom been driven in the intervening couple of years.

It was a Sunday morning, and so Michael Enright's voice came through as the *Sunday Edition* was broadcast. Enright's voice was lulling, soft, and fatherly. The announcer's voice was one that Michael had always enjoyed. The episode was a summer rerun, one that Michael had heard in part before.

He drove past a cabin—a rural house, really—where kids were running around in the front yard, near the road. He slowed down. The kids all stopped mid-run, watching him as he passed—so he waved to them. The smallest, a boy of perhaps eight, waved back. Michael remembered being such an age, remembered a time when the summer, when the sheer play of it, felt like an extended forever.

A few minutes later, Michael arrived at the grocery store with its conjoined liquor store in the back. It was busy out on the asphalt parking lot—it was a summer's weekend day. He imagined what the traffic must be like on Highway 2 right now, the artery that pumped north and south between Calgary and Edmonton. He ducked into the store, grabbing a pen from the glove compartment: Michael was partial to completed tasks, to crossing items off a list.

The air inside was cool and dry, the crowd large and pleasant. People seemed to be lively today, excited, happy to be there. Michael got a grocery cart and began loading up with what was on the list. On a whim, he decided that he would cook them all a meal—a large, rich, satisfying feast.

He began to plot what it would be. He looked over the store and checked his options. After gliding up the aisles and down—seeing bottles, bags, produce, and packages—perhaps improbably, even to himself, he settled on duck: there was a selection of them in the freezer. He chose two, along with a heap of the less ordinary vegetables—parsnip, fennel, celery root—alongside the potatoes and greens that they had for many cabin dinners. He would make the feast tomorrow, he reasoned, for it was already too late to thaw the fowl.

He continued along through the aisles, picking the foods that he knew everyone enjoyed, in addition to what was on the list. He stopped through the liquor store as well, adding a case each of white and red wines, as well as a case of beer, as the cabin was getting close to being out of most things.

Clare had given Michael her credit card, for which he found himself grateful, if a bit embarrassed. He could only have afforded to pay by adding the bill to his significant debts, though, and his mother knew it.

So he swiped the card, forged the signature, and walked out of the store, back into the bright sunlight of the warming day. He passed a well-dressed family on their way in as he headed out. They were loud, laughing, and the younger ones were racing into the store. One of them almost bumped into the cart.

For a moment, Michael was irritated, but then in the next he wished that his family were more like that: more raucous, with more *joie de vivre*. Perhaps, though, that was simply what he wished for himself.

There were no significant messages in his inbox, and the drive back was equally uneventful. Michael Enright and his radio interviewees kept Michael company. There was an interview with an historian whom Michael had chanced to meet the previous year. He had missed part of the interview last time the episode was aired. It was satisfying to hear it through this time. Another something completed, filed away.

Michael had thought the historian pompous at first, but then she had turned out to know who he was, which had amazed him—it was on account of his supervisor's good word, he had imagined. She had encouraged him to stick with his work, something that had buoyed him up more than she could have known.

He enjoyed listening to this interview now, catching it all this second time. He passed John and Benjamin again as he returned to the cabin, and this time he honked at them. Shave and a haircut. The old horn of the pickup wheezed out louder than he would have expected.

*

John and Benjamin had been out for a solid two hours. They were both glad to be arriving back at the cabin. Benjamin was especially glad, as he was suffering much more than he was letting on, even though John had slackened his usual pace a great deal. They were walking now, cooling down, not saying much, but happy for each other's company.

Although John would not speak much of it, he had witnessed terrible things in Afghanistan. He had been responsible for ending the lives of other human beings. It was as if the horror of his old dreams had come true—and more, given the extended duration of his service. In the perched high plains, he had witnessed desperation and lawlessness unlike anything that he could have imagined.

His official diagnosis was post-traumatic stress disorder. Shell shock. This news he had shared with the family.

Clare had felt hurt—it was a deep injustice that her son could be so wounded by the decisions and actions of the state! She coddled him now, held him to her heart, perhaps too much so.

She also saw to John's being kept in company. They all did.

Benjamin enjoyed being with his cousin well enough, enjoyed it better than ever, but in the past he would have left John alone to his runs.

Yet it was good for him: between the dog and the baby and the house and the job and the daily cares of life, Benjamin had seldom, of late, taken the time to take care of himself. The neglect was taking its toll on many fronts. He had huffed along beside John, who, although six years older, was in far, far better shape.

John had indeed witnessed horrors overseas. They came to him now, as they did often. While the immediate object of being there had seemed clear enough, at least from afar, the daily situation on the ground had made little to no sense to John.

On the one hand, this other world had given him perspective. The most pressing of his cares in the past were a mere trifle to what he had seen every day. On the other hand, between the roadside bombs, the bouts of being under fire, and the gut-wrenching, destroying recognition that—after the longer timeline was considered—they were contributing to a long history of colonial invasions, John found himself wizened, a little bit black in his soul.

He had seen friends, colleagues killed, too. One day, in a moment that he would recall with vivid clarity until he recalled no more, on a sunny day not dissimilar to the bright August in which he and Benjamin were now walking, they drove through a small village not far from Kandahar on patrol. A sudden blast had flipped their vehicle, torn it into shrapnel and left it a burnt-out husk.

John had been—somehow—unhurt beyond bruises and scrapes. He remembered his expectation, as the dust began to clear, that they would be under further attack. They all expected that the blast would be followed by rounds fired by unseen attackers.

Yet there was nothing: the dust cleared, and the sun was still bright overhead. He remembered that he was in command. There was no one else near them. The village had left them alone, let them risk their own necks.

So there was no one else about. He stood up in the dust and the remnants of the vehicle and began to check the others. His mind went over protocols. By and large, they were going to be okay. There was a sliced open arm here, some shrapnel wounds there, and the force of the impact for all.

As John looked into the vehicle, however, he saw what he could tell right away was a body.

He approached and saw a man who, until a few moments ago, had been a Master Corporal whom he had known for three years, a man from Antigonish with a family waiting for him at home. Some flying piece of the wreck had gone straight into his skull, just under his helmet and near the back of his neck. At least the death had been a quick one, but the sentiment was a horrible cliché that brought no closure.

It was the first death on John's command. It was the first death that he had witnessed up close, too. He remembered the dead man's eyes. John wondered what daily cares, what worries, had vanished in the moment of his death—and what beauties, what things that would never be remembered again.

What things will disappear and be lost from the world forever, the moment that we depart from it?

John was noted for his actions that day. He had radioed in, and there had been no further problems.

Two years later, another man from their unit, a man from Portage la Prairie, who had ended up losing his lower arm after that day, took his own life.

Now, John remembered the clear panic, the feeling of being alone with his experiences. He would discuss these thoughts with his therapist and no one else. He did not wish to frighten his family with his thoughts, with his sudden flashes of what it would be like to be knifed in the abdomen, or of how easily a skull could be crushed.

So, instead, John tried to focus on the other things about being overseas. With his conscious mind, he thought about how kind many people were, or about how there had been a Tim Hortons on the base, or about how inquisitive and shy the local children had been.

What he endeavoured not to think of was the terror of how little separated this world from utter wreck and collapse.

Yet his thoughts, his thoughts haunted him. How could he move on from his knowledge? How could he balance his desire to bring peace to the world, to help others through his strength, with Canada's warlike turn?

John was trying to find this balance at a slow pace, as his therapist counselled. Healing was not immediate. He was, so far, unmedicated, declining the SSRIs and Ativan that he was offered. However, he could not dare miss his runs—or his newfound meditation practice—for to do so led him off a sharp cliff and into nightmare fantasies and recollections that he could not bear.

That these would fade, as his therapist told him, was his only saving thought when things were at their worst, when he wanted to end them.

He was, too, ordered to spend as much time with family and friends as he could. These actions—being with his kin and comrades—were to reground him. The goal was to free John enough from the past to start, once again, to plan a future. Yet, after all of the years that had passed, his only real friends were now those with whom he had served. Even those links were tenuous, frayed by the terror of experience. They were friends who brought bad memories to the surface when they were together. As a result, they drifted, eddied, apart from each other.

So here he was, as ever, with his family.

They did not know how much they were saving him, John thought.

*

Benjamin had little idea, for instance, of how much he might be saving John as he walked along beside him, the sweat pooling at the base of Benjamin's spine. He knew that his cousin was hurting—that much he could tell—and it was enough.

Benjamin was hurting, too. In his case, though, the pain was by and large physical. He hadn't run this much in years, if ever. The pain was compounded by lifestyle, he knew. He tried to get to the gym—he did, he tried—but it happened seldom enough that on most weeks he did not get a proper workout. He was exhausted, exhausted in a way that he hadn't known existed until now.

Yet, Rebecca, with her master's degree, was the one who found herself staying at home with their baby, taking Max out in their very expensive space-age aluminum alloy stroller with hydraulic suspension while walking the dog.

Even though Benjamin continued to work, and so in that sense his life was uninterrupted, and his career would progress—he could even continue to train and to upgrade his certifications—they shared night duty. It was Rebecca's progress that was interrupted, but they had reasoned that her staying home with the baby was an easier choice and, somehow, an equitable one, too.

Benjamin had changed so many diapers in a somnambulant state that some days he felt that he no longer knew where the boundary between sleep and wakefulness lay. He was exhausted. He was bone tired. In all probability, he was a hazard to himself and to everyone around him. Coffee helped to regulate his waking hours, but it added to his nighttime restlessness.

And so. So: these days, he appreciated his parents in a way that he never before had done. That anyone could give her very consciousness over to the maintenance of the life of another human being was something that he found quite marvelous. Rebecca was patient, so very patient, from everything that he could observe. That one might simply expect this work from people, women, mothers, every day, was astonishing.

And so: he was in awe of his parents, really for the first time, as well as of his wife.

But he knew that he had to rest, had to cease at some point—and he had to take better care of himself. He had to rest before something bad happened, or before he did something genuinely stupid as a result of sheer exhaustion and stress.

There were days when he felt anger flare up inside of him, a deep rage that he did not understand or recognize. So far, he was able to govern his frustrations, but he knew that he needed to care for himself, too.

The run, in short, did him good even though he was suffering, and it would lead to days of aches.

The two cousins said nothing to each other as they came up the drive, back to the cabin: they didn't need to.

Once, they would both have run down to the lake and jumped in, all mirth and irreverence. Now, they felt tired.

No one told me, Benjamin offered, that these years would be so hard. He sighed, kicked the gravel.

Well, said John. He paused. I suppose we might not have come along for the ride had we known. The sentiment sounded darker than he had intended, yet it hung there still. I mean, I suppose it lets up eventually, doesn't it?

John didn't know, as they entered the cabin again, through the basement door. Did it let up? Did his own self-recriminations let up at some point? Would he begin to forgive himself for those whom, along the way, he had hurt, let alone those who had died under his watch? At what point could he let go of the pain in his heart and let the past be? Every moment that he did not, he felt—he knew—he kept the present from ever being true for him. He did not allow the future to grow. He was stuck.

What was worse was that his feeling of being stuck just added to the problem. He had been down this path before in his thoughts, many times. Life seemed to be irreconcilable with itself. But the problem also seemed to be just a little bit less urgent now than it had been.

John sighed too, heading inside.

Benjamin and John parted: Benjamin for the upstairs bathroom, John for the basement shower.

It felt quiet inside, entering in the basement, and it was: Jéanne, and Françoise were down at the shore. The twin sisters were reading on the sands. Doug and Mike were soon to be getting out the canoe. For the moment they were upstairs. There was a hush inside.

Michael was in the kitchen, putting away the spoils of his trip to town. He was also preparing lunch—and setting in motion his preparations for the supper that he had planned for tomorrow.

Daphne, Celeste, Rebecca, and Max were in the basement, playing with the baby and the dog. It was a time of day that worked well for the baby: he lolled and drooled on himself: he was merry while his mother and his two young aunts tended to his needs like fawning servants.

The dog would come over and lick Max's face every now and again, which the baby found to be hilarious. Sarah was a stinky cocker spaniel with an improbable name. At two, she was very active.

Max laughed and laughed.

His mother shooed the dog.

Celeste and Daphne praised the child.

On his way to the shower, Benjamin kissed Rebecca and chucked Max's chin. He climbed the stairs—these seemed to be just a little bit, well, difficult in these tired days—and went into the bathroom, closing the door behind him.

*

Clare, in the living room, saw Benjamin and John enter. She listened as, a moment later, the water began. She was in the living room—she was reading Proust.

Still! But it was complicated. Perhaps the fact spoke to her perseverance and not to her failure.

She could appreciate why it had taken several translators to get Proust right—and why the text then needed to be edited all over again anyhow. She moved through the process of reconstructing memory, of finding a path, a path back to mother, a path to something lost that one could never in reality hope to retrieve.

Like her dear William. Alas!

She wept still some nights, alone in what had been their bed. She had thought that perhaps she should sell the house in the city, because every corner was imbued with William's fading touch. In Elbow Park, it would sell very well—she would do well if she sold it.

Yet how could she! For her sons needed still to have a home to come back to: John was staying at home now, while he convalesced: Michael, though he was keeping his apartment in Toronto, was in a poor financial situation, she knew. Perhaps he, too, would end up back home if his search for work did not take him in a more fruitful direction soon.

It would be a comfort to have them both at home! Clare thought. And yet, she knew that hers was a selfish desire—she knew that her sons needed to be sent out into the world. Again.

She shifted, working on her own sense of memory. She thought of walking in the city, on 4th Street, on 17th Avenue, in Inglewood, in the spring. She had spent so much time in these parts of Calgary. Her life was bounded by, perhaps, Glenmore Trail to the south: the reservoir. The Elbow River to the east. 14th Street—or maybe Marda Loop—to the west. Kensington or perhaps 16th Avenue to the north, but even that was a stretch. Life in and around the Elbow and Bow rivers: that was home.

The house was not in Mount Royal—William had not been quite as successful as that!—but it stood nearby on a tree-lined street. Mission was a comfortable walking distance, and she had watched the neighbourhoods change over the years.

The city had changed, too, it had grown up—as she supposed they all had. Calgary's inner southwest was staid, bourgeois, and refined. The art galleries represented very good artists—or at least very expensive ones. She still enjoyed the neighbourhoods, the city. The philharmonic was good, as were the theatre companies.

She remembered being a young woman in the city, with the man who would become her first husband, Daniel. The sense of untapped, undeveloped potential. The gaudy, garish displays. These were still there; the city seemed to be all but unchanged under its shiny new surfaces, a maverick mindset still lauded at City Hall and among the city's elites—for the city had always had a professional class that ran it all.

She wondered what future version of the city—of the cabin communities, of the lakes, of Canada—her sons would live on and into.

She turned to Proust.

*

From the table, Mike felt Clare's attention stray, wander, and then return to the book. While it was early in the day, he and Doug were already immersed in a game of Risk. They told themselves that it was a prelude to getting the canoe out—a sociable way of drinking more coffee before they would need to paddle.

Mike rolled the dice—six, four, two—and dispatched two of his brother's troops in Kamchatka. Eastern Russia had become the crux of this game.

Surely they all should have learned by now, from William's beloved Napoleon if nowhere else, Mike thought: never start a land war in Asia. Yet how often we repeat our mistakes if we are not mindful. Mindfulness was on Mike's mind a great deal now.

He rolled again, lost two of his own troops, and had to break a larger piece down into singles.

After all of these years, he and Jéanne had realized that their best chances for happiness were with each other. He didn't resent Jéanne her time away, nor the lovers she had had. Theirs had been a slow reconciliation, a delicate process borne first of the necessity of negotiating their parenting lives, then later emerging from a dawning recognition that the world either would not or could not offer them anything more than that which they would find in each other.

The world, in the end, was a disappointment. In each other they found comfort.

Mike rolled, claimed Kamchatka, and poured his troops across the border. Yakutsk was next: Doug had not defended it well. These were all territories that had changed hands several times. Françoise had held them early on, when she was still in the game.

Mike did not regret the time that he and Jéanne had been apart, at least not anymore. It was the past. Yes, sometimes it stung—he could admit that much to himself—but to call it regret was not quite right.

He made a practice of meditation now. He was very much able, after a good sit, to recognize how his moments of hurt were based on ego, based on a fixation upon a self, an idea of a self, that was fleeting, passing. His transience grounded him and let him relinquish the past.

Doug felt the change in his brother. So much was gone from his arguments, or rather had changed: Mike now seemed to like to find points of agreement and to build upon those. The practice, if he was frank about it, annoyed Doug, who continued to like a good debate.

He could still get his brother going, though. How, for instance, would Mike reconcile his newfound inner peace with his bellicose enjoyment of Risk?

For Mike was making a run for it, a calculated gamble that looked like it would lead to his victory—or ruin. Doug lost Yakutsk, Irkutsk, Siberia, China, and Siam in rapid succession. Mike already held Australia, New Guinea, and Indonesia. He turned his attention westward.

Doubtless Mike would have some answer about the game being a thought exercise if Doug challenged him.

Mike's forces were still going strong, but he left only a single piece in each territory that he conquered: he would be hopelessly thin on the ground if Doug could stop his progress. India fell in a few rolls.

It would come down to the Middle East.

Doug admired his brother's seeming peace these days, though: Mike was less likely to interrupt, to speak over others. He was seldom one to drink too much or to offend others. But then, also, he was less likely to laugh. On the balance, the change was welcome, though Doug wasn't always sure.

It would come down to the Middle East. Doug rolled a five and a six in defense, killing two of Mike's troops.

Mike did seem happier, at any rate. Doug had to grant and respect that much.

*

Jéanne, who had been eliminated from the game without further ceremony when her ex- and future husband had conquered Madagascar, passed by, heading for the deck. Her irritation with the game had been brief—she expected it. She and Françoise had only joined in order to humour Mike and Doug.

Jéanne smiled at Clare, who looked up from Proust. Then Jéanne opened the sliding door and went outside, where her sister was enjoying the August sunshine.

I must get W—or, rather, someone—Clare thought, to fix that door!

Outside, Jéanne wore a pair of large, black sunglasses that she had purchased in Istanbul three years prior. Her sister, she saw, had neglected to wear her sunglasses.

They had both aged—they saw it in each other. Jéanne was thinner now, the skin on her upper arms, in particular, vexing her as it hung in ways that it never used to do. Their bodies still treated them well enough—they both walked a great deal, they both did regular yoga—but they could see, and now acknowledge, that they were becoming old.

Françoise had allowed her hair to grey, and it looked good on her. She was now a handful of years—four, she hoped—from retirement, and she had taken on the thankless task of chairing her department.

Her department had now become an odd assortment, a clutch of fields in the arts housed under one chair for mere administrative expediency. A mélange of disparate disciplines that bore the aftertaste of bad coffee and early morning meetings. Émigrées and émigrés from other, former departments rubbed shoulders with one another in frustration. It felt like an uncomfortable mix of desserts and savouries, sweaty cheeses left too long in the sun, all paired with wine from a box.

Nevertheless, she bore her role well, wore the mantle of mid-level academic leadership with all of the world-weary expressions that were necessary to stave off the worst of the cuts and to keep her colleagues content enough.

With but a few years left to go, however, she realized that she would not publish another book until retirement. The special issue of the journal that she had edited didn't really count—she had finished it some time ago, and it was a small enough project, truth be told. Only so much could be done while chairing.

Jéanne understood without her saying so that Françoise's role was onerous. For her part, she had come to enjoy her past few years of finding herself and was getting set to contribute to her community in a new way, although she hadn't quite figured out how, not just yet. Perhaps she would work with some friends who laboured to support refugees.

She wanted to begin, though, by providing some more direction to her daughters. Celeste was on her way: since she had completed her education program, she had managed to find steady work. Teachers who spoke French were in demand in Alberta—and Celeste had so far been lucky, too, beyond that.

Now, though, at twenty-six, Celeste needed some guidance to take her next steps beyond her career.

Daphne was more of a concern, however, not having found anything that truly inspired her. But she accompanied her mother in anything asked of her and had a big heart. Jéanne felt that her separation from

Mike had had its greatest effect upon their eldest. It had seemed somehow to freeze her in place, to paralyze Daphne's ability to make life-changing decisions, beyond having moved to Calgary for work.

But by now, Jéanne knew, that could not be helped. The only direction was forward, because that is how time seems to work.

She chose the chair next to her sister, who pulled down her book—she had been using it to block the sunlight, not really reading it—and closed it, placing a bookmark inside. Jéanne was pleased to see that it was a mass-market paperback and not some serious academic piece.

It was hot on the deck. They sat there and sweated.

It was both strange and welcome to have rediscovered Mike. Jéanne had dated and had had one-night and multi-night stands while travelling, while discovering her new life. The experiences were fleeting and infrequent. She had been lonely in that time.

Mike had focused on work—he was engrossed by work and had kept himself distracted with it. He had paid her support. Had he been waiting for her to come back? He said that he hadn't ever expected anything—that he had sought to rid himself of expectations—but Jéanne couldn't help but wonder.

Nor had they slid back together as though by old habit: they were still tentative around each other, making sure that they still drank coffee, checking on how they took their coffee these days. Trust once ruptured was slow to be established anew.

The children did seem pleased, perhaps Benjamin in particular—Benjamin who seemed to be doing well, though, of course, he had those years of intense career and family struggles ahead of him, Jéanne knew. She supposed that it simplified things for the children, things like the holidays. Perhaps it meant more than that—the children did seem keen to see their parents' relationship succeed.

For, in the end, there was Mike. He was loyal. He was kind at heart, if sometimes rough around the edges, his legal mind not always hung up at the door. Mike, who had a good sense of what he liked and, after all, had learned that he liked her. He wasn't perfect, but he was nonetheless the best.

And isn't that what it means to live well? Jéanne asked herself. We live imperfect lives, but whatever they are, they are always, necessarily, the best lives possible.

There was Mike, after all.

And now here he was, sliding onto the deck.

Game go well? Jéanne asked.

As well as it could, Mike said, with a bit of a non-committal shrug. I was wondering who was doing the dump run. Thought I might ask the girls to come with.

The truth was that Mike was a little bit restless. Perhaps he and Doug should get the canoe out now—but they had agreed to wait on it until a bit later. Were there any chores that needed doing? He thought that he might ask Clare.

Why don't you just let the girls go? Jéanne suggested. They can handle it. Might be an adventure.

Oh! I hadn't thought of that. Of course—why not?

For he hadn't. Of course they could: they were licensed, they drove, and it was a simple enough task.

Why don't I go down and ask them, Mike said.

Then he was gone, leaving the two sisters there in the sunshine.

Mike went back inside, shedding his sandals at the door, and went downstairs, where Daphne, Celeste, and Rebecca were still playing with Max. They seemed to be loving the situation—and to be a bit forced in their enthusiasm, all at once.

Mike made the suggestion: his daughters looked at each other.

Actually, Max is just about ready for his nap, Rebecca said. It would be perfect timing. We're lucky he hasn't cracked already.

Rebecca was finding her voice more and more with the family, although it had taken some time. Celeste thought that it had happened since her sister-in-law had become a mother. Circumstances forced her to speak up for herself as part of advocating for the baby.

Daphne would have said that it had happened when Rebecca was pregnant—she had suffered so much from nausea throughout that she had just run out of patience and made a decision to advocate more often.

Whatever the reason, Rebecca was decisive now: she picked Max up and headed to the bedroom in order to get him down for his nap.

*

Daphne and Celeste were happy enough to take on their father's suggested task, even if they were a bit unsure of themselves. William, after all, had done this work in the past—and it had always been taken on by one of the men since his death.

Celeste remembered how she had gone once when she was young, along with Helen—but that was over a decade ago now. Still, it would be an adventure, and it had the benefit of helping the cabin to remain a quiet place during Max's nap.

They followed their father upstairs to find the keys to the truck and to get their shoes, and then they headed outside to load up the truck. None of the work was demanding, though the dump run did seem like a bit of an unusual task to the women.

What a strange and troubled world it is, Celeste thought.

Daphne drove—she was the more comfortable of the two behind the wheel of a truck, they decided. They rolled down their windows and let the warm afternoon air pass through the vehicle's cab, the August leaves rustling along the margins of the country road.

The load was not huge, but it was large enough. It was late in the visit. There remained tonight, and then tomorrow after supper most of them would decamp, with just John, Michael, and Clare left for one night longer. Those three would take care of the end-of-summer cleanup, the last bag or two of garbage coming with them back to the city. So the box of the pickup was more or less full of bags of garbage, the collective detritus of their summer retreat—diapers and foodstuffs, packaging, and things that had broken down along the way.

The two sisters chatted at first as they drove, catching up one-on-one. Celeste's teaching, which exhausted her, left her very little time to run the rest of her life, she found. Almost the only thing that Celeste did beyond work and the quotidian necessities—but this she did not share with her sister—was write. She wrote stories that she kept to herself, all of which featured protagonists named Helen. These Helens were not her lost cousin, but a variety of women named Helen. Each lived a different life at a different station along the path. Celeste wondered, fretted, over whether her scribbling had any merit. But it was, after all, just for herself, she reasoned.

Daphne's life in Calgary—she worked for the municipality now, an administrative job connected to City Hall that paid well enough and was a good jump from her previous employment. The job allowed her to continue avoiding having to make decisions about her life. She was about to turn thirty-one, though, and beginning to feel some pressure to get on—well, to get on with something, anyhow.

Though that wasn't really her way. .

So they chatted.

This is the land of our defeat, Daphne said.

What, are we lost? Celeste answered. Have to inquire the way?

They had both studied Canadian literature at university, and they dropped into sharing references with each other. They had, as they studied, discussed texts, sent things to each other that they liked. Although in different classes, they had been taught from the same anthology and had read many of the same books.

A fish hook, an open eye, Daphne said, switching poets. Nope. I remember the way. I could always turn on my phone—it has GPS. But I'm much happier with it off when we're up here. A right turn at the next stop sign, and then it isn't far now.

At this moment, Celeste ran out of words.

*

It wasn't far, as Daphne had said. The old truck rattled to a stop, turned right, headed down the road for a period of time, the roadside grasses disturbed by the wind that was pulled along by the Chevy.

Then they arrived at the turnoff to the dump.

And what was this? The dump had changed since Celeste had been there last. In fact, the access road was closed, the dump with it. Several signs had been added to the fence. Your home on Natives' land, read one. Stolen land, read another.

There were two police cruisers at the turnoff, lights spinning. It was the rail crossing that was blocked. An officer waved them along. Beyond them, protestors were set up in the afternoon. There were flags flapping in the light breeze. The scene was quiet. There was a détente.

Celeste read the protestors' signs of solidarity. Now what? she said.

I don't know, was all that Daphne could offer.

They two women sat there in the truck, looking at the gates, the rail crossing, the signs. They looked further, into the dump, the piles of refuse. The silent bulldozer. The trailer that had housed the operations of the dump looked empty. Surely there had been something in the news? How had they missed it?

Do you remember, Celeste asked, how much Helen loved the dump?

Yes, of course, Daphne answered. She always came back with stories. Especially stories of bears. I think she would be okay with this, though.

There was also a bears-in-area warning at the turnoff to dump, but the sign was faded, a permanent fixture with rusted buckshot holes. The fences still stood to deter the bears, as well as the deer, but the bears were nonetheless a constant risk, knowing as they did how to find a way in.

I think, though, that what she really liked about it was the chance to be with Uncle William, Celeste added.

Yes, Daphne agreed.

It's hard to believe that they're both gone, Celeste observed.

Yes, Daphne said anew.

They fell to a quiet, driving slowly past in the truck and looking into the empty dump, the heat of the day, the trees all around, the blockade, the signs, their unknowing. An RCMP officer waved them on.

The time I came here with them, Celeste said at last. I remember Helen being so disappointed that there were no bears that day. But there were crows in the trees, as well as gulls. I hadn't really noticed, but Helen turned to look at the birds, seemed to greet them like friends. It wasn't the same as bears, but it was a nice trip. I've always enjoyed the smell of the truck, ever since—I remembered that day when we opened the doors.

Well, said Daphne. What's left of it. Daphne wasn't quite sure how to respond to her sister: there was something a little bit embarrassing about the sentiment, but only in its honesty. A direct acknowledgement—or worse, a question, a request for something more—would render that embarrassment explicit.

What next? Daphne asked.

Celeste shrugged.

The truck inched along, closer now to the tracks, the fencing of the dump visible just beyond. Foxtail grew in a small drainage ditch. Their windows were open. Gravel from the shoulder crunched under the tires. The protest was in their rear-view mirror, the flashing lights as well.

Just then, both women heard a deep huffing sound, a snuffling from the other side of the fence. They turned to look. There, in the shadows of trees at the dump's edge, and kept in sharp contrast by the sun overhead, they saw a black bear. She was good sized, and not far away. She looked at the sisters. They stopped the truck—the bear was less than fifty metres away, separated from them only by a length of simple chain link. Through the trees, they could see that the mesh was down on the other side of the dump. That must have been how she had gotten in. Such fencing would not keep a determined bear at bay. Surely the others, a few hundred metres back down the road, knew that she was there?

The bear harumphed. Her black fur shone where the sun struck it. She stuck her nose into the air, smelling the world around her. Then she looked at Celeste and Daphne.

Behind her, Celeste could see a cub—no, two cubs—following their mother's lead. They were young cubs, paying more attention to each other than to anything else.

Daphne spied them, too. It must have been because of the shade from the trees that they took so long to notice them, she thought.

The cubs paused. They looked at the truck, at the women. And they looked right back. Time seemed to suspend itself. Insects buzzed in the warmth.

After a moment, the encounter was over: the mother, the sow, harumphed again and turned, heading for the downed fence and back into the trees. The cubs turned and followed her.

Celeste and Daphne were left in the sunlight, sitting in the cab, wondering what to make of it. Celeste, wearing an old, plaid flannel shirt and ripped jeans, now felt exposed, disarmed. Daphne wiped a hand on the edge of the worn-out T-shirt that she had found at the cabin, a shirt from some charity 5K run many years ago. Taking their time, they put the pickup in gear.

*

I do like this old truck, Daphne said, by way of saying something reassuring. I'd never buy one or anything like that, but I'm glad it's here. It's nice to drive, too. Rolls over anything.

The sun glared off the windshield as they bounced along the path back to the main road.

It's something constant, Celeste agreed. I can't imagine the cabin without it, even if it's really not an important piece of my life. I'm glad it's here, too.

They were both, however, thinking about the bears, about how their fur gleamed in the sunlight, and about how their cousin would have been so pleased by the auspicious encounter. The protest, leading to the undelivered garbage, nagged at their minds, but it couldn't be helped for the moment. They did not know what role they could play in it. The gulls wheeled overhead, a raven cawed across the nuisance grounds, and a woodpecker hammered away at a bough in the forest.

They drove along in silence, the August heat climbing, the cab reaching the point of being sweltering as they regained the main road. Daphne figured that simply heading back to the cabin was best. The late afternoon provided a crescendo to the day's temperature. It was hitting a fortissimo.

With the windows down, they could hear the asphalt rolling below, the leaves catching the breeze thrown up by their passing, insects buzzing. They made the left turns that were necessary to get back, rolled up the gravel of the drive, and pulled the truck up to its appointed spot beside the garage.

*

As they drove, Celeste worked out the details of a new Helen story, one that had been giving her trouble for some time. Her window down, she watched the trees pass, heard the crickets and the birds, but did not register them as Daphne steered them back to the cabin.

The story was set not too far from where she had lived in Toronto during the end of her studies, on Wellesley. In it, Helen was a woman in her late thirties, divorced, and isolated in spite of living in the heart of the bustling city. She imagined that the world was more brilliant than it really was, a world in which the sidewalks shimmered as though encrusted with diamonds, rather than reflecting sunlight off the shards of the broken bottles of cheap vodka.

Helen was unable, though, to fall in love, and this part Celeste couldn't sort out. Perhaps it was that her childhood had been too fanciful, and that nothing in adult life could compare. Her first marriage had happened quickly and ended just as fast, when her husband left her to go and travel in Tibet. Helen had lovers, but they all left her after a while because they knew that she could see a diamond-filled world and they weren't in it. Helen looked at the clouds and saw dragons. Her partners looked up and saw only the rain that was coming and said that they'd better get indoors.

The story, Celeste figured, revolved around the barbershop where Helen got her hair cut once a month. Helen dealt with the banal, everyday world in which she completed boring tasks for money—where she worked a government office job—by establishing routines that left her free to live in the better world of her imagination. Her barber, who had a Spanish name like Jorge or Luís—Celeste hadn't yet decided—was a kind, gay man who enjoyed life in Toronto's Church Street village. His hands were firm, yet soft. He wore a leather apron and was unapologetic. He was, however, a little bit sad around the edges of his mouth and in the growing creases of his eyes. His hair was greying, and he was, alas, becoming too old to continue to live the same life he had for all these years.

Helen came to see Luís—maybe that was the right name—every month, without fail, and she began to open up to him, sharing with him the fanciful things that she saw, like the flock of geese that spelled secret messages to her as they veed across the sky. When she first opened up, she was worried that she had embarrassed herself: a grown woman who refused to grow up, like an amphibian that refused to leave the mud and take a step on dry land. She even missed one month's appointment.

But Luís surprised her by hanging onto every word. Celeste smiled as they drove now, imagining this part of the story. Luís was also heartbroken from failed relationships, and Helen's vision let him know that there could be more to the world than he had believed. It restored his optimism. She restored his optimism.

From there, the story didn't have enough structure yet. It had its fairytale elements and was another of Celeste's Helen stories, but she thought that it could be perhaps the best that she had written if she kept at it. Helen and Luís would, over time, develop their own sort of love—or at least care—for each other. Luís' dissatisfaction would be remedied, in a small way, by the stories that Helen brought to him, like the time the pigeons on the power lines wrote out the score to "Ode to Joy," their bodies marking the notes on the wires. Or the story of the time Helen stumbled across a meeting of raccoons who were comparing the things that they had stolen from the city's pawn shops. Helen, in turn, realized that none of her lovers could match Luís' keen eye for detail, the precision with which he fixed her hair, each time, into the perfect bob, as he listened to the stories that she told, and as he lived his beautiful life.

In time, they would realize that, although they were incompatible, they nevertheless loved each other in a fashion. They moved in together, never had babies or even tried anything as absurd as sex, but, once a month, Luís cut her hair, and Helen brought home the stories that she collected, which were like the shiny things that she saw all around herself, everywhere that she went.

Celeste could see it all, now, all of a sudden, and just had to write through to the finish. She held onto her vision as they re-entered the cabin.

*

It was getting to be late in the afternoon. Inside, dinner preparations were being made for the evening meal. Down at the lake, Celeste and Daphne found Benjamin, Rebecca, and Max. The dog, Sarah, was there, too. She was running along the dock and contemplating the water—as well as the strange behaviour of the humans who were wading in the lake. She looked to be timing the right moment for her entry to join them.

Rebecca and Benjamin were attempting to demonstrate to Max that the water was not a place of deep existential horror: Max was terrified of the water. He was having none of his parents' cajoling and was climbing up his mother, yelling and wailing. But he seemed to calm down a little at the sight of his two aunts.

Weird to think of ourselves like that, as aunts, Celeste thought. Yet so we are.

No one spoke at first. Here they were: all these years later, and the three siblings stood at the same shoreline. Benjamin was wading in the same muddy shallows. They were playing in the same sandbox as ever, protected by the same spruce, pine, and aspens.

Celeste looked across the water, into the trees, and contemplated the word tamarack.

And Max makes our parents into grandparents, Daphne knew.

Benjamin wondered if his sisters would become parents, too. He knew it was up to them, but he also wondered if Max would have cousins and siblings to play and to fight with. There would already be an imbalance between the generations: Max was to be the oldest and, at this rate, would be the oldest by a stretch.

In their generation, John was the oldest, but only by a bit, and they all—the five of them who were left—clustered tightly together. Grapes in a bunch. Peas in a pod. The next generation would be different and would have its own pressures.

Would it matter that the next set of their family would be different? Benjamin couldn't help but feel that the shift marked some sort of failure.

Well, come on then, Rebecca said, show Max how it's done.

Oh, said Daphne. Right, yes, of course.

The sisters sat down on the shore, rolled up their jeans, took off the shoes that they had worn on the failed trip to the dump. Celeste got up first. She stepped along the flats and into the shallow water.

Daphne followed. The water was warm—she relished the feeling of the lake mud oozing between her toes—and she stood for a moment, feeling her digits squishing the muck.

Max turned to look at his aunts, his eyes widening to see two more adults walking into the water of their own seeming free will.

Sarah barked and yipped and then returned to running back and forth.

We want him to get a feel for it, Rebecca said. He'll start his first swim lessons this fall.

Max decided at length that his aunts' behaviour was acceptable. He smiled and began to reach for Daphne, his small hands gesticulating, his fingers opening and closing like a crab's pincers as he tried to communicate his desire.

Rebecca waded over and handed Max to her sister-in-law.

Careful, sweetie, his mother said to him.

Hweeeee, answered Max, spitting. As soon as Daphne held him, he began to thrash about—she lowered him into the water—he thrashed some more.

This play went on for some time. None of them spoke in any significant way to each other—the conversation was all directed toward Max— words of encouragement and instruction.

Soon Daphne and Celeste were soaked through. Celeste gave in: she threw herself right into the water, jeans and all, for Max's enjoyment. He burbled.

Ashore, the dog cocked her head and continued to be puzzled by the humans, by their laughter, by the strange ways in which they used their energies, the strange things that they taught the baby (who had learned nothing so far of sniffing, fetching, or hunting). The baby was the crux of the dog's interest, for the dog watched over young Max with as much care as any of the adults did. Max was more Sarah's responsibility than anyone else's in her view.

Now, though, was Sarah's moment. Running back a small distance, she circled and then leapt into the lake. She charged into deeper waters. She then began a swim in Celeste's direction. The humans laughed. Max clapped his hands as he laughed also.

In time, interest in the activity wore itself out. After sunning themselves on the shore and on their towels, everyone returned to the cabin. They joined Clare, Mike, Doug, Michael, John, Jéanne, and Françoise for dinner. Michael's two ducks were thawing, out of sight, for tomorrow, and everyone enjoyed a meaty barbeque, the twelve of them the largest summer party that they had had there in some years.

Both tables were again joined together, wine was poured, and the day flowed into the night like a gauze or a shawl descending to muffle a lamp, to cloak the corners of the cabin. There were games, conversation, and all.

Late into the night, Clare climbed, alone, into bed. The bed was cold. She stretched her toes into each of its corners. She was sad, but she liked the chilly sheets.

Tomorrow and tomorrow and tomorrow, she mouthed to herself, turning out the light.

She wondered for a moment if she shouldn't get herself a new dog. In the basement, she could hear the occasional rumble of the television in the Other Room.

*

By the morning, however, Clare's mood had cleared. She renewed her resolve never to replace Mackenzie.

What a hassle he had been as a pup! she recalled, yet again.

It was cool out, though warming. The bushes rustled with squirrels and hummed with shade-loving insects. She met Françoise and Jéanne on the deck: each of them had a coffee in hand. Clare wore a familiar light blanket from the living room on her shoulders.

The women sat in silence for a time, sipped.

I never know anymore, Jéanne offered by way of conversation, what to do with myself when there are no pressing concerns. The children do not need me—my labour-time is free—and while I suppose I could do some cooking or some cleaning, I don't have to.

This is, of course, only a problem of privilege, her sister countered. In most places in the world, you wouldn't even be asking yourself the question.

Yes, yes, of course—in some ways, that's just it, Jéanne continued. In many other places in the world I would already be dead, too. During all the years of raising children, of minding a house, of curating a life—let alone the years of separation—it was always clear, more or less, what I had to do next. In fact, for a long time it was more than I could do, and I always felt like a failure. Now there is time enough, but I find it hard to enjoy. I feel like a failure for not enjoying it enough, and I feel the inequality not just of money, but of time, too.

There was a pause before Françoise replied.

I have to admit that I am somewhat afraid to think of my retirement. I know how to fill the time, but I can also see how arbitrary any of my choices are. Volunteer my time with women fleeing violence? Sure, but why not homeless youth? That I can even ask such a question is perverse.

The thought hung in the air.

Well, after all, Clare said, we have become obsolete. She thought of William as she gave voice to a long-held thought that he had been fond of expressing. Let our children decide what to do now. I, for one, plan to take up painting.

It was true: Clare was enrolled in a watercolour course back in the city that would begin in September. She would see how far that would take her.

It's cost me a few years, she added, but I am slowly growing to love the space and time again.

I fear it will never be like when we were young, though, Jéanne said. When there was time enough to be bored, when it stretched itself ahead of me in a hazy, open sort of way, when I didn't need to think of what, exactly, would happen next. It was a void—it wasn't even something that I could have begun to formulate as a question or as an issue.

Already I'm slowing down, Françoise said. I can see my colleagues expecting my departure from the university, see them getting ready to argue about how they can best replace me, reallocate the funds of my salary—the fiction that my salary would somehow stay in the department. It's just as I would have done in the past, before I was at this point. I wish I'd been more compassionate.

Well, Clare suggested, you can join me in my painting. Write another article, another book. Enjoy the victory.

Yes, Françoise conceded. And yet: it isn't the same when you no longer have to prove yourself. No one else cares anymore.

Which is why you have to discover how to care for it yourself, her sister rejoined. Learn who you are on your own terms, not someone else's.

The conversation tapered, and all three women sipped their coffees. Françoise was indeed planning another book. She thought of it now. It was something that was so far indistinct, but that swirled around the idea of the human, how the very idea of the human failed us—how it failed people in different ways. The concept was as yet diaphanous, gossamer, a volume that revealed itself in small flashes like a beacon casting a glow at intervals through the darkness.

They turned to discussing other things: friends, medical conditions, the cares and concerns of the younger generations. Through the trees and down at the water, they could hear the children—and Jéanne's grandchild! Clare thought to herself. It was, yet again, a clear August day, and Françoise was glad to hear them down there, taking advantage of the sunshine before the weather grew too warm.

*

As with the day before, Benjamin and Rebecca were attempting to teach Max that water was not a site of the unknown, that it was not the abyss clawing at his heels. This splashing was the noise that Clare, Françoise, and Jéanne could hear from the deck: that, and Max's uncertain yells and hoots.

Max's aunts were prepared this time: they had brought their swimsuits and were waiting in the sun. Benjamin took a turn with Max, took him to the edge of the water, where he sat him on the sand. Benjamin took two steps back into the lake, watching Max the whole time.

Sarah bounded up to the edge of the water and stared, as did Max.

Benjamin reached down into the water with his arms, reaching for the bottom. He made a face at Max, a scrunched-up face of comic uncertainty, but then stopped as Max's own face began to evidence worry rather than mirth.

Then Benjamin stood up, lake muck in both of his hands. He smeared it on himself and then laughed.

Max laughed too, a laugh of relief, seeing his father model the behaviour. Benjamin then went down for more muck, and this time went over and smeared it on his son. Max looked shocked, at first, and then continued laughing.

Rebecca looked on, not knowing if it would be too much. But all would be alright: Max was laughing: he was content. It was enough to break the fears wide open—Max pulled at the mud on his body, threw it into the air.

The dog ran for cover and all of the adults laughed. Max began to crawl toward his father—his mother came over to take him into the lake. She set him down in the shallows. Once in the water, he sat up and began to reach down for clumps of muck. Rebecca watched over him, expecting him to fall face-first into the water.

Plus ça change, Daphne said. I think I'll swim.

Me too, Celeste said. It's been rather a long time, after all.

And, indeed, it had been: with the onset of adulthood, the children had seldom done such things. It had been, what, five years since Celeste's last swim of any length?

What is it that I have been doing? Celeste wondered.

She couldn't say, but the clocks continued to turn: the world moved on, and she felt refreshed and restored by the passage of time itself.

She found herself trailing her sister, who was doing a very competent breaststroke toward the dock. Celeste's hair fanned out in the water. She found that it was getting in her face as she swam. She floated along, then, less concerned about reaching her goal.

Perhaps life was like that, she thought: she had reached the goals—at least, the professional ones—that she had set, and now she bobbed along. How long could she just float there? Daphne, on the other hand, swam. Was that what it was like? Celeste couldn't tell.

Part of her mind floated to a recent Helen story that she thought she might have finished, a historical narrative set around the time of the First World War. It had involved a large family and the tragedies that they endured. Then she drifted to another one that she had enjoyed, a contemporary one with a young protagonist named Helen who had invented roller sliding, the dangerous sport of roller skating on abandoned waterslides.

But now Daphne arrived at the floating dock, which really did seem like it was closer than it had been. Celeste could see her sister pull herself up and onto the dock and stand in the sun.

Her sister was indeed beautiful, Celeste recognized, but in the same instant she knew that she was beautiful, too. She bobbed along. Soon enough she also arrived.

*

Celeste pulled herself up the ladder that extended three rungs into the water and stood on the fake grass, the cheap astroturf that covered the surface, about three metres on each of its equal sides.

The gulls, for whatever reason, had never seemed much to like this square of itchy plastic, so it remained more or less shit-free.

I'm sure it used to seem further, Daphne said.

Her mind cast to an imagined time before now in which the shore was but a speck on the horizon from this dock, a land that she spied like a sailor through a glass, distant and unclear.

They looked toward the shore, to their brother, his wife, and their son, still mucking about. They saw their cousin, John, returning from his run, and his brother, Michael, walking toward the shore, a book in his hand.

Behind them, their father, Mike, was ambling toward the lake with Uncle Doug, too. The two men turned, however. They headed to the boathouse—really just a canoe shack, Celeste thought to herself.

Daphne could tell from their clothes and their gear—fishing tackle, beer, and a bag of food—that they were going for a longer paddle today.

Fantastic weather for it, Daphne thought.

Up above, gulls were wheeling in the drafts as a few clouds scudded past, different layers moving at different speeds.

As she watched her father and uncle prepare the canoe, the realization dawned on her: Daphne knew that she would have to unleash herself. For everything here at the cabin was a repetition. They were all comfortable in their routines—the running, the canoeing, the walks, the food, the wine—though maybe no longer the dump. It was good, but it was unremarkable.

What had she accomplished? She had a bachelor's degree from McGill to show for her time so far, and that had ended six years ago. She was nearly thirty-one—many artists had made their mark by their age, and many athletes had retired. An artist like Basquiat was already four years in the grave.

She had survived her perilous twenties by staying quiet, by behaving well, and as a result having a string of disinteresting work to show for it, right up to her time at City Hall. She knew of passion—she had had partners—but she chose a quieter life in the Beltline and lived in a modest apartment. She loved walking along the rivers, seeing the people wandering with their babies and their dogs—but she did not make the same plunge, did not take the risks that, she felt, she would need to take in order to get something more out of life.

Why was she so taciturn? She felt anxious to step out of the boundaries that she knew, but she could feel the necessity of doing so—of surprising her family and her clutch of friends by stretching out into the world.

It dawned on her: she was waiting for permission before transgressing any of the silent boundaries that she had set for herself—but she needed no one's permission but her own. She held all of her family in such respect that she was always ready to help anyone in distress—but, she saw, that meant that she also held them at a bit of a distance. Everyone was in the habit of describing her as being old before her time. She realized, however, that she had just not yet been young.

As she watched her father and Doug begin to pull the oars, she wondered—worried—for a moment—about the consequences—but then realized that she was already living with the consequences of her inaction. She remembered the concluding lines of a book of poetry she had read. Go forth and undo harm. Go forth and do.

She ran, plunged off the dock with a speed that she had never mustered before, and opened her eyes underwater. What was she seeking? Was it others' recognition? Did she want something only from a vain sense of ego? Or was it, rather, an awakening to the potential to do something—finally, to do something—that might make passage through this world a bit gentler for those who would come after?

The green of the lake was pierced by flashes of sunlight, light that reached down into the deep that dropped into a silent gloom. She watched the light playing, began to let it take on a symbolic register.

Looking to the left, she saw the slice of the hull of the canoe, then the paddles moving through the water. She came up for air, then went down again, into darker water, where—perhaps for the first time—she felt both at home and able, with a little effort, to break free. Shafts of light descended, sparkled in the emerald water that faded into jade depths.

Daphne floated up and treaded water, looking back at her sister, who was still on the astroturf of the floating dock. Celeste was beautiful, she knew, but was she growing a little bit pinched? Was that what the relative security of being a teacher did to one—pinched and puckered one's eyes? She had resented her sister's sure path at one time—the calm way in which Celeste had set about building herself a life while Daphne didn't even notice how she was doing so—and yet, now she didn't know which would be the better way of learning to grow into one's adult skin: with the assurance of a limited, professional mien—or with the open honesty of a failing, a flailing, and a flawed human body.

Yet she could see that she had so far refused even this choice. Celeste at least had chosen. Daphne felt her heart swell up with a sudden freedom, opened by the decision ahead of her. The heart would ache at times, yes, but at least it could feel!

Celeste watched her sister swimming, her fluid, confident strokes in the lake. These days, she felt afraid of the water. Not afraid in any serious way, nothing to be concerned about, she thought: it was just an undercurrent. She knew that she was beautiful, still—she loved her own hair and her own skin, after all—but more and more these were becoming cold comforts.

Something pulled from underneath. She envied, she knew in her heart, Benjamin's son, the fact that her brother had a son. She wished that she did not have this envy, but she did, best social critiques of the bourgeois family be damned. She grew tired of being single, tired of the restraint with which she lived every day.

How free Daphne looked just at this moment!

But Celeste knew, or felt, that it was all a part of growing up—growing up in a serious way this time, growing into a profession and a life, not just asserting one's independence upon reaching the age of majority. She wished that someone would acknowledge all that she had done to get to where she was.

But her sister looked so free. Could she herself feel so free? Could she embrace the water in the same way? She paused, held herself there.

As she did so, Celeste watched the canoe paddle past, saw her father and uncle push out from their little nook of the lake and out of sight around a corner of land, behind the stand of spruce that stood upon the point.

They vanished, sliding into the unknown, a mystery pointed toward the future.

We'll be back in time for supper! Already around the corner, Mike called back to his daughter from his seat in the back of the canoe.

To Celeste, these felt like the words of the dead, haunting words returning from a land that she could not see, could not access or know. The words floated in the air above the water, dispersed, insects dotting the surface of the lake.

Doug paddled onward.

For his faults over the last few years, Celeste thought, her father was good in his heart. She was glad to see her parents reunited, she had to admit to herself, though she was unsure what to do with her own reencounter with them. Now her parents were not simply the grownups in charge, but were instead flawed people with embodied wants, needs, and desires. She knew both of her parents' weaknesses now, as well as some of their depths and complexities. This new knowledge surprised her, even scared her some.

*

A couple of years ago, Mike wouldn't have trusted himself to steer the canoe: he would have feared being in charge, being responsible for the position. Today he had hopped in the back, forcing himself to take charge. He had steadied the boat for his brother.

Even if he had to put it on somewhat, to act the part, Mike reasoned, he could rediscover confidence if he put himself to the task. He longed for a smoke. Mind over matter. Matter over mind? He felt like if he worked at it, he would be strong again. He was getting there now, after all.

The boat slid along the lake. Doug had noticed the change in positions, of course, but had gone along with Mike, not wanting to question or ask. He appreciated the steps that his brother took to put his life back onto the track that he wished for himself. Doug was a good paddler and was happy to provide the pull that the canoe wanted for its trip, the small prow cutting through the gentle waves of the lake.

Mike and Doug kept the canoe running along the shoreline, perhaps as much as a hundred metres from shore. Their path lay, at first, to the northwest. They paddled in silence, the warm day heating up, the sun climbing overhead.

The cabin's corner of the lake was a quiet one: other cabins dotted the lakeshore, more or less spaced out, small docks jutting into the deepening waters.

Each cabin offered a new set of appearances: this one was brown, with pink chairs—the next one was a cabin in light blue vinyl siding—the next one white aluminum with a longer dock of weathered wood. Doug noted each, was familiar already with each from past paddles. He thought about their visual aspects, what they could offer to a photographer. Anyplace else, they could be deemed homes. They were houses, really. Cottages, if they were in Ontario—chalets, if they were in Quebec.

Different boats were tied up in front of the cabins: some cabins had large powerboats and gear for waterskiing and tubing, while others had canoes, kayaks, upturned on the shore. They passed a cabin with a plastic yellow pedal boat, flipped over on a stretch of beach. Then a large, wood-beamed cabin that loomed up from the trees.

Mike steered, paddled: Doug pulled them along, thinking about how he had still not read Proust.

At length, the lake turned more to the west. Mike looked back from where they had come.

Seems small from here, Mike said. An indistinguishable corner. He strained his eyes.

And yet, his brother answered. It was ever thus, he added in his thoughts.

They paddled on for a stretch, now approaching a marshy expanse from whence the lake drew its waters, from the gentle creek that emptied into its expanse, after pouring down mountain slopes further westward. No cabins were here, and, early in the season, this patch of the lake was best avoided, as it was home to swarms of mosquitoes. By this time in the summer, however, the mosquitoes were in check, as the dragonflies and birds feasted on the insect life among the reeds.

Out on the open waters of the lake, a motorboat roared toward them, then banked, whipping an inner tube with a teenage child across its wake. Further out, the sound of outboard motors was part of the August background hum.

The reeds and the grasses, though, were peaceful. Bulrushes stretched skyward. Looking over the edge of the canoe, Mike saw water striders stepping across the meniscus of the water. He marvelled still at the gentle nature of the insects' walk.

A large blue dragonfly settled on a stalk of marsh grass nearby.

They could hear the distinct call of red-winged blackbirds throughout this wetland. A bird flew into view, a warbler, which then flitted back into the trees.

The brothers remained silent, bobbing in the grasses, sitting, calming themselves in the sunlight. Upon close inspection, the grasses broke down into different types of reeds and rushes.

As the waters around them stilled, the sun began to shine into the green depths, striking the bottom of the lake, which lay some two feet below them now, a green murk of algae and mud.

In spite of the human activity—in spite of the gasoline and the oil—this lake still seemed to be healthy enough, Doug estimated.

A small school of fingerlings swam through the patch of pond into which he was looking. Further into the lake, the larger fish lazed in the middle depths.

Mike thought of the fishing gear in the bottom of the canoe, but it wasn't the best time. Mornings and evenings were the time to fish: anytime much after dawn, right through the afternoon, was a time for calm. Perhaps the mood to fish would strike them, but, then again, it might not.

Doug could read his brother's thoughts. So much depends, he murmured to himself.

*

Looking out from the windows of the cabin toward the lake, Michael shared his uncle's sentiment. The sun had crested, and it would start to descend.

So he hadn't managed to make much of his career yet: let it fall short. Let him fail. He would learn, he would make his peace. He resolved that this would be his last semester of multi-campus commuting.

There were other things to do. Like cook the ducks that he had decided upon for the evening. He was going to give them an orange glaze—duck à l'orange was the only thing that he could think of when it came to duck. So what the hell—he would make it.

Instead of potatoes, there would be parsnip, carrots, and fennel root—or whatever it was that he had bought. It wasn't that he felt the food at the cabin was inadequate: rather, he just wished to take on a domestic challenge that he knew he could enjoy. He would make a turnip soufflé to go with it, and a cake, a chocolate fondant.

Michael began to make several things at once. The cabin was quiet.

His mother and aunts were still on the deck, each absorbed in either reading or napping, there being but a blurry line between the two states of being. The first hints of shade were being cast by the nearby trees as the sun's angle shifted.

His uncles were out there somewhere in the canoe, perhaps fishing, perhaps polishing off a beer or three.

Everyone else seemed to be down by the lake, though he thought that he might have heard someone come in downstairs a while ago, either to use the bathroom or perhaps to have a nap.

The cake. Michael mixed ingredients in two bowls, adding dry to wet, and getting the batter into a pan, into the oven. He would need to free up the oven to get the ducks in, let alone the root vegetables.

It was a mercifully large oven, and Michael realized, again, that it was very impractical to be baking and roasting on such a summer's day. Could he cook the meal on the barbeque? He'd never tried roasting on one: he would have to ask and he didn't want to do so.

He would need a salad to go with the duck, too—that was where his thoughts led him.

He took more things out of the fridge. So he was impractical. If he were practical, if he were ruthless, he would already have turned the dissertation around, gotten his book out. Then perhaps fuller employment might be on the table, instead of just root vegetables. As it stood, he had the half-hearted interest of a second-tier academic publisher, a few articles, and a teaching schedule that kept him from getting much done.

Michael prepared ingredients. The gentle, meditative washing of lettuces. The scrubbing of carrots. The quiet concentration of the cutting board. Things began to pile up.

Michael felt that his career looked much like his progress in preparing the meal thus far: many ingredients, but still no duck à l'orange. He ducked back into the fridge to bring out the fowl, which he would start to dress next.

He was aging, Michael knew—aging into the disappointment of not being famous, of not being terribly interesting. Of calming down, too, though. Friends and lovers had come and gone. He believed that he was at his core a good person, but he was no longer as fervent in his beliefs. He felt that he had misstepped, too, and more than once.

When he was younger, he mused to himself, he believed in revolution. He believed that his belief in revolution excused everything that he and his comrades did—to themselves, to one another, to the world. They were perfect then. And terrible. Their compromises were never real, just temporary expedients that would be done away with when the walls fell.

Michael thought of the rallies that he'd helped to organize, protests on campus. His peers in the union.

He still believed in revolution, he went on, just to himself. But he had spent the past few years apologizing, making up for the past. No revolution without accountability.

Michael debated—he was often debating with himself nowadays— whether he had sold himself out, or whether he had just begun to realize that he was imperfect: that his past wasn't just one of calling out injustices, but was one of participating in injustices, too, often at the same time. Simply by virtue of being here, on colonized land. Simply by occupying the position that he did.

He knew that it was an irresolvable quandary, but that didn't equal a good excuse.

He sliced carrots on the cutting board, watching the sun move through the sky, and prepared a heartfelt meal for the family who, he knew, loved him in all of his flaws.

*

H was a wall.

H was a cupboard.

H was a house.

H had four walls on the inside.

You had to cut out the cardstock in order to build H, like one of those old models of the Parliament buildings or of the CN Tower.

H was a corridor.

H was a poet.

H was your bare thigh caressed by your lover's tongue.

Jéanne woke from her daydream, from her reverie, with a start. Her book had fallen on her chest. She picked it up, but realized that she would in all likelihood nod off anew. It was warm on the deck.

*

Outside, John was away from the others. He had wanted some quiet as the afternoon slid away into evening. Everything seemed so much calmer, so much slower, back at the cabin, back in Canada.

He could not tolerate the pace.

Part of him was still convinced of the need to be on the alert, to maintain vigilance—to assume that any moment could be the moment of his death. That was of course always true, but had little of the same immediacy here. His feelings were, in other words, out of place. He no longer knew how to govern them.

On the one hand, he thought as he walked, he had spent a long time mourning, regretting, even, his childhood choices and the difficult times that he had endured overseas. But he saw a path ahead.

He could live a lifetime of quiet regret, or else he could persevere. To be open to the future, open to the potential that he still felt within himself, he would need to choose a different path. It was a path of new choices, of making new choices. He had started. He had contacted his old girlfriend and apologized again, across the years. His youth was a scar that he carried with him, and it itched, scratch it as it might. It would not heal on its own. Perhaps it shouldn't. She had accepted his new apology and did not ask for more. They had agreed to let the past be the past.

It was unsatisfactory, yet it was all that he knew how to do. The past was impossible, and yet so was the future without it.

To make new choices, he realized, would be to honour those who came before him, those who had died in recent memory and those who were longer gone: his sister, his uncle, his father—even old Mackenzie. And then before them, his grandparents, the Briscoes, the MacDougalls, and the lives extending into the beyond of what he knew, of what he could see.

He crunched in the undergrowth and lifted a branch that had fallen, that hung at waist height across the almost indistinguishable, overgrown path. For all of the changes, he could say that he remained here, to honour himself and those who had come before. If his actions had not always been the best, that did not make him a bad person, he reasoned. Such a concession would be death. His faults, rather, made him what he was. He would remain. He would be better than before.

Still here—he was still here, so many years later. He had, after all, endured, stayed still. Could he say that this one place was, in some sense, his as a result? No. And yet, here he was.

Pushing through the trees, John moved away from the lake and into the undergrowth. His feet stirred up the remains of an old life jacket, long worn out, the yellowed foam sticking through faded blue nylon. He kept moving. He saw the glint of the canoe heading back, caught the sound of laughter at the water's edge. He headed in that direction. He was here, still.

＊

On the deck, Clare heard the tromping of John's shoes in the bushes. For a moment she mistook the sound for William. Looking off the deck, she thought: this was the view that her husband had loved! Then her mind slid to meals, to the next day, and to the day after that. She thought of the sound of bare feet padding across a tile floor. She thought of dried mud on a different floor. She put her book down and looked, past Françoise and Jéanne, to where the sounds carried in the light August breeze. Jéanne was resting now, her book beside her: her eyes may have been closed behind her sunglasses. Clare couldn't tell. Françoise was reading with seeming determination in her deck chair, a slight frown on her face. How alike, yet utterly different, the two sisters were! Clare thought. Her mind spun in the afternoon, landing on the idea, the ideal, of a life that added up to something greater than itself. She remembered her childhood, how her parents, too, had struggled but not given up. It was, she decided, enough.

Acknowledgments

We Are Already Ghosts draws inspiration from many texts and authors. While the ones who inform the spirit of this work are bpNichol and Virginia Woolf—especially Woolf's novels *To the Lighthouse* and *Between the Acts*—the text includes a wide range of allusions from William Shakespeare to Karl Marx to Gertrude Stein and beyond. Permissions have been sought for materials covered by copyright. A brief excerpt of this book, entitled "For the Last Time," was published by No Press in 2018; my thanks to derek beaulieu. "Springtime in Vienna" (Baker, Rob / Downie, Gord / Fay, Johnny / Langlois, Paul / Sinclair, Gord) copyright © 1995 Little Smoke Music c/o Southern Music Pub. Co. Canada Ltd. Copyright © Renewed. Used by permission. All rights reserved. Lines quoted from Al Purdy, "The Country North of Belleville," *Beyond Remembering: The Collected Poems of Al Purdy*, edited by Sam Solecki (Harbour Publishing, 2000) are quoted by permission of Harbour Publishing. "You Fit Into Me," from *Power Politics*, copyright © 1971, 1996, 2018 by Margaret Atwood, is reproduced with permission from House of Anansi Press, Toronto. www.houseofanansi.com. A line from bp Nichol's *Dada Lama* is reprinted with permission of the estate of bp Nichol. The line "Go forth and undo harm. Go forth and do." Comes from *Expressway*, by Sina Queyras, published by Coach House Books (2009), and is reproduced with permission.

This book was completed in Calgary, Alberta, the city in which I live, but it was also written in Montréal, Quebec; in Salamanca, Spain; Banff, Alberta; and Cortes Island, British Columbia. Thank you to my hosts in each place: Will Straw at McGill University in Montréal; Ana María Fraile Marcos at the University of Salamanca, Spain; derek beaulieu at the Banff Centre for Arts and Creativity; and Naava Smolash on Cortes Island. Thank you to everyone at the University of Calgary Press, and in particular Helen Hajnoczky, Brian Scrivener, and Aritha van Herk. My gratitude to Naomi K. Lewis for the attentive and thoughtful editorial process.

While the lake on which the novel is set is fictitious, it draws inspiration from the lakeside communities of south-central Alberta, and Sylvan Lake in particular, where I have spent considerable time. This region lies in Treaty 6 territory, a treaty signed in 1876 between Cree and Nakoda nations and the British Crown and is home to many Indigenous peoples. I live in Treaty 7 territory (1877), in southern Alberta. My settler family's roots and routes cross the territories of treaties 6, 7, and 8 (1899), and I endeavour to work in the spirit of treaty in my works and life.

There are many who held up this work beyond those whom I am able to mention here; thank you all. Thank you to my colleagues and friends at the University of Calgary and at Mount Royal University. My profound appreciation for early readers Gregory Betts, Rohanna Green, Aubrey Jean Hanson, and Naava Smolash. Encouragement from Marie Carrière was important to me. Conversations with Gala Arh, Archana Rampure, Kate Siklosi, Bart Vautour, and Erin Wunker were a tremendous boost. Marie-Andrée Bergeron and Emma Gibbons: to you both, my most profound appreciation and awe.

We Are Already Ghosts is written with gratitude for my grandmother, June, my parents, Keith and Debbie, as well as family members Beth, Simon, Patti, Bruce, Jesse, and Dan. This book is composed with an eye toward the generation of young people around whom I am privileged to live: Alexandra, Clementine, Emma, Thomas, Ambrose, Wynn, Adelaide, Baxter, Louis, and those yet to come.

For Aubrey, as ever.

Photo Credit: Ashley-Rae Photography

KIT DOBSON lives in Calgary, Treaty 7 territory, in southern Alberta. He is the author or editor of eight previous books, including *Malled: Deciphering Shopping in Canada* and *Field Notes on Listening*, one of the CBC's top non-fiction books of 2022. *We Are Already Ghosts* is his first novel.

 **BRAVE & BRILLIANT SERIES**

SERIES EDITOR:
Aritha van Herk, Professor, English, University of Calgary
ISSN 2371-7238 (PRINT) ISSN 2371-7246 (ONLINE)

Brave & Brilliant encompasses fiction, poetry, and everything in between and beyond. Bold and lively, each with its own strong and unique voice, Brave & Brilliant books entertain and engage readers with fresh and energetic approaches to storytelling and verse.

Printed by Imprimerie Gauvin
Gatineau, Québec